THE RAVISHING
OF LOL STEIN

MARGUERITE DURAS

. . . .

THE RAVISHING OF LOL STEIN

TRANSLATED FROM THE FRENCH
BY RICHARD SEAVER

PANTHEON BOOKS, NEW YORK

All rights reserved under International and Pan-American Copyright Conventions. Published in the United States by Pantheon Books, a division of Random House, Inc., New York, and simultaneously in Canada by Random House of Canada Limited, Toronto. Originally published in France as *Le Ravissement de Lol V. Stein* by Editions Gallimard. Copyright © 1964 by Editions Gallimard. This translation first published in the United States by Grove Press, Inc., in 1966.

Library of Congress Cataloging-in-Publication Data

Duras, Marguerite.
The ravishing of Lol Stein.
Translation of: Le ravissement de Lol V. Stein.
I. Title.
PQ2607.U8245R313   1986   843'.912   85-43441
ISBN 0-394-74304-0

Manufactured in the United States of America

468975

For Sonia

Lol Stein was born here in South Tahla, and she spent a good part of her youth in this town. Her father was a professor at the university. Lol has a brother nine years older than she—I have never seen him—they say he lives in Paris. Her parents are dead.

I have never heard anything especially noteworthy about Lol Stein's childhood, even from Tatiana Karl, her best friend during their school years together.

On Thursdays, which was a school holiday, they used to go out and dance in the empty playground. They had an aversion to marching in schoolgirl file with the others, and preferred to remain back at the school. And they knew how to get their way too, Tatiana said, they were a beguiling pair and knew, better than the other students did, how to solicit that favor and get their teachers to grant it. Shall we dance, Tatiana? A radio in a nearby building was blaring a medley of old-fashioned tunes—a program of nostalgic favorites—which were all they needed. With the monitors gone, alone in the vast school courtyard where, that day, between dances, they could hear the street noises: Come, Tatiana, come, let's dance, Tatiana, come on. That much I know.

This too: Lol was nineteen when she met Michael Richardson one morning during summer vacation, at the tennis courts. He was twenty-five. He was the only son of well-to-do parents, whose real estate holdings in the vicinity of Town Beach were considerable. He had no real vocation. Their parents consented to the marriage. Lol must have been engaged for six months, the wedding was to take place that autumn, she had just finished her final year of school and was on vacation in Town Beach, when the biggest ball of the season was held at the municipal casino.

Tatiana does not believe that this fabled Town Beach ball was so overwhelmingly responsible for Lol Stein's illness. No, Tatiana Karl traces the origins of that illness back further, further even than the beginning of their friendship. They were latent in Lol Stein, but kept from emerging by the deep affection with which she had always been surrounded both at home and, later, at school. She says that in school—and she wasn't the only person to think so—there was already something lacking in Lol, something which kept her from being, in Tatiana's words, "there." She gave the impression of being in a state of passive boredom, putting up with a person she knew she was supposed to be but whom she forgot about at the slightest occasion. The epitome of thoughtfulness, but also of indifference, people were quick to discover, she never seemed to suffer or be hurt, had never been known to shed a sentimental, schoolgirl's tear. Tatiana still maintains that Lol Stein was beautiful, that they vied for her affection at school—although she slipped through their fingers like water—because the little they managed to retain was well worth the effort. Lol was funny, an inveterate wit, and very bright, even though part of her seemed always to be evading you, and the present moment. Going where? Into some adolescent dream world? No, Tatiana answers, no, it seemed as though she were going nowhere, yes, that's it, nowhere. Was it her heart that wasn't there? Tatiana apparently inclines toward the opinion that it was perhaps, indeed, Lol Stein's heart which wasn't—as she says—there; it would doubtless come, but she, Tatiana, had never seen any sign of it. Yes, it seemed that it was in this realm of her feelings that Lol Stein was different from the others.

When the rumors of Lol Stein's engagement first began to be heard, Tatiana only half believed them: who in the world could Lol have found who was capable of capturing her attention so completely?

When she met Michael Richardson and saw how madly Lol was in love with him, Tatiana was completely taken aback. But there still remained a lingering doubt: was this not a means whereby Lol was ending the days when her heart was not yet touched completely?

I asked her if Lol's subsequent illness was not proof positive that she was wrong. She repeated that it was not, that she, personally, believed that this crisis and Lol were but one and the same, and always had been.

I no longer believe a word Tatiana says. I'm convinced of absolutely nothing.

Here then, in full, and all mixed together, both this false impression which Tatiana Karl tells about and what I have been able to imagine about that night at the Town Beach casino. Following which I shall relate my own story of Lol Stein.

As for the nineteen years preceding that night, I do not want to know any more about them than what I tell, or very little more, setting forth only the straight, unadulterated chronological facts, even if these years conceal some magic moment to which I am indebted for having enabled me to meet Lol Stein. I don't want to because the presence of her adolescence in this story might somehow tend to detract, in the eyes of the reader, from the overwhelming actuality of this woman in my life. I am therefore going to look for her, I shall pick her up at that moment in time which seems most appropriate, at that moment when it seems to me she

[handwritten margin notes: "obsessed w/ facts" and "jibe to Tatiana – she brings in adolescence"]

first began to stir, to come toward me, at the precise moment when the last arrivals, two women, came through the door into the ballroom of the Town Beach casino.

The orchestra stopped playing. A set was just ending.

The dance floor had emptied slowly. There was no one on it.

The older of the two women had paused for a moment to glance around at the crowd, then she had turned back, smiling, at the girl who was with her. Beyond any shadow of a doubt, this girl was her daughter. They were both tall, both built in the same way. But while the girl displayed a certain awkwardness because of her height, and because of her somewhat angular build, her mother, on the contrary, bore these defects like the emblems of some obscure negation on the part of nature. Her elegance, both when she moved and when she was in repose, was upsetting, Tatiana maintains.

"They were on the beach this morning," said Lol's fiancé, Michael Richardson.

He had stopped, he had watched the new arrivals, then he had steered Lol toward the bar and the cluster of green plants at the far end of the room.

The two women had crossed the dance floor and headed in the same direction.

Lol, rooted to the spot, had watched, as had he, the advance of that careless, slightly-stooped grace of a dead bird. She was thin. She must always have been thin. She had clothed that thinness, Tatiana clearly recalled, in a very low-cut black dress, with a double layer of tulle over it, also black. This was the bearing and the clothing she desired, and she looked exactly the way she wanted to look, unquestionably. The admirable bone structure of her body and her face showed through her skin. As she thus appeared, so later would she die, with her desired body. Who was she? They later learned: Anne-Marie Stretter. Was she beautiful? How old was she? What had she, Anne-Marie Stretter, experienced that other women had missed? By what mysterious path had she arrived at what appeared to be a gay, a dazzling pessimism, a smiling indolence as light as a hint, as ashes? A certain self-assured boldness was all that seemed to hold her upright. But how graceful it was, as was the woman herself! Their loping, country way of walking would keep the two of them in step wherever they went. Where? Nothing more could ever happen to that woman, Tatiana thought, nothing more, nothing. Except her death, she thought.

Had she looked at Michael Richardson as she passed by? Had this non-look of hers swept over him as it took in the ballroom? It was impossible to tell, it is therefore impossible to know when my story of Lol Stein begins: her gaze—from close-up one could see that this defect stemmed from an almost painful discoloration of the pupil—was diffused over the entire surface of her eyes, and was hard to meet. Her hair was dyed red, the sun had burned her red, a seaside Eve whom the light did not do justice to.

Had there been a glimmer of recognition when she had passed by him?

When Michael Richardson turned around to Lol and asked her to dance for the last time in their lives, Tatiana had noticed that he had grown suddenly pale, and was so completely lost in his own thoughts that she knew that he too had looked at the woman who had just come in.

Lol most certainly noticed this change. She was, it seemed, transported in the presence of this change, without fearing it or ever having feared it, without being surprised, as though she were already familiar with the nature of this change: it affected the very person of Michael Richardson, it was related to that person whom Lol had known up till now.

He had become different. It was obvious to everyone. Obvious that he was no longer the same person they had thought he was. Lol was watching him, watching him change.

Michael Richardson's eyes had grown brighter. His face had tightened into the full of maturity. Pain was etched upon it, ancient, primordial pain.

The moment they saw him again this way, they knew that nothing—no word, no earthly act of violence—could have the least effect upon the change in Michael Richardson. That it now had to be played out to the bitter end. Michael Richardson's new tale had already begun to take shape.

In Lol, this vision and this conviction did not appear to be accompanied by any sign of suffering.

Tatiana herself found Lol changed. She watched

and waited for what would come next, brooded over the enormity of it, its clocklike precision. If she herself had been the agent not only of its advent but of what would come of it, Lol could not have been more fascinated by it.

She danced once again with Michael Richardson. It was the last time.

The woman was alone, standing slightly off to one side of the buffet, her daughter had gone over to join a group of acquaintances near the door to the ballroom. Michael Richardson made his way over to her, prey to an emotion so intense that they were frightened at the very thought that he might be refused. Lol, in a state of suspense, waited, waited like the others. The woman did not refuse.

They had walked out onto the dance floor. Lol had watched them, the way a woman whose heart is wholly unattached, a very old woman, watches her children leave her: she seemed to love them.

"I have to invite that woman to dance."

Tatiana had seen him act in this new way, had seen him go over to her, as though in real agony, bow, and wait. She had frowned ever so slightly. Had she also recognized him, from having caught a glimpse of him on the beach that morning, and for that reason alone?

Tatiana had remained at Lol's side.

Instinctively, Lol had taken a step or two in the direction of Anne-Marie Stretter at the same time Michael Richardson had. Tatiana had followed her. Then they both saw: the woman's lips parted ever so slightly, but no words emerged, overwhelmed and

awed as she was by the new expression on the face of
the man she had but glimpsed that morning. The
moment she was in his arms, from her sudden awkwardness and her benumbed expression, caught and
frozen as she had been by the rapidity of it all, she too
had been overwhelmed by the same feeling of con-
fusion which had taken hold of him, Tatiana had realized.

Lol had gone back behind the bar and the cluster of
green plants, Tatiana with her.

They had danced. Danced again. He with his eyes
lowered, fixed upon the bare part of her shoulder. She,
shorter than he, simply gazed into the distance at the
ball. They had not exchanged a word.

When the first dance was over, Michael Richardson
had come back over to Lol, as he had always done till
then. In his eyes was an imploring look, a call for help,
for acquiescence. Lol had smiled at him.

Then, at the end of the following dance, he had not
come back to Lol again.

Anne-Marie Stretter and Michael Richardson had
remained together the rest of the night.

As the evening wore on, it seemed that the chances
that Lol might suffer were growing increasingly slim, it
seemed that suffering had failed to find any chink in
her armor through which to slip, that she had forgotten
the age-old equation governing the sorrows of love.

In the first light of dawn, when night was gone,
Tatiana had seen how all of them had aged. Although
Michael Richardson was younger than this woman, he
had overtaken her, and together—with Lol—all three
of them had aged years and years, grown centuries

older, that kind of age which lies lurking, within the insane.

At about this same time they spoke, exchanged a few words while they danced. But between numbers they continued to remain completely silent, standing close together, apart from all the others, always the same distance. With the exception of their hands, which were joined as they danced, they had not moved any closer together than that first moment when they had exchanged glances.

Lol was still in the same place, behind the green plants at the bar, where she had happened to be standing when Anne-Marie Stretter entered.

Tatiana, her best friend, still there too, was stroking her hand, which lay on a small table beneath the flowers. Yes, it was Tatiana who had offered her this gesture of friendship throughout the night.

With dawn, Michael Richardson's eyes had searched for someone at the far end of the room. He had not found Lol.

Anne-Marie Stretter's daughter had long since left the ball and gone home. Her mother, it seemed, had not noticed her leave, or missed her presence.

Doubtless Lol, like Tatiana, like the couple themselves, had failed to take into account this other aspect of the matter: that with daylight it would come to an end.

The orchestra stopped playing. The ballroom seemed virtually empty. There were only a few couples left, including the one they formed, and, behind the green plants, Lol and that other girl, Tatiana Karl. They had failed to realize that the orchestra had stopped playing: after the break, at the moment when it should have started in again, they had moved back together, like robots, deaf to the fact that there was no longer any music. It was at this point that the musicians filed past them one by one, their violins enclosed in funereal cases. They had made a motion as if to stop them, perhaps to speak to them, but in the end they did not.

Michael Richardson wiped his forehead with his hand and scanned the room for some sign of eternity. Lol Stein's smile, then, was one such sign, but he failed to see it.

For a long time they had stared at each other in silence, not knowing what to do, how to emerge from the night.

It was at this point that a woman well along in years, Lol's mother, had entered the room. Insulting and reviling them, she asked them what they had done to her child.

Who could have informed Lol's mother about what was taking place that night at the Town Beach casino? It could not have been Tatiana Karl, Tatiana Karl had not left Lol Stein's side. Had she come on her own?

They glanced around, to see for whom these insults were intended. They did not respond to them.

When Lol's mother found her child behind the cluster of green plants, a tender, plaintive moan flooded the empty room.

When her mother had reached her side and had touched her, Lol had at last let go of her grip on the table. It was only then that she had realized, vaguely, that something was drawing to a close, without quite

knowing what it might be. The screen which her
mother formed between them and her was her first
inkling of it. With a powerful shove of her hand, she
knocked her mother down. The vague, emotion-filled
wail ceased.

Lol cried out for the first time. Then, once again,
there were hands around her shoulders. She surely had
no idea whose they were. She would not let anyone
touch her face.

They began to move, to walk toward the walls,
searching for imaginary doors. The half-light of dawn
was the same indoors and out. At last they had found
the way to the real door and had begun to move slowly
toward it.

Lol had gone on screaming all sorts of things that
made perfect sense: it wasn't late, it was only the early
summer dawn that made it seem later than it really
was. She had begged Michael Richardson to believe
her. But as they kept on walking—they had tried to
prevent her but she had wrenched free—she had run
to the door and hurled herself against it. The door,
latched to a jamb at floor level, had resisted her efforts.

With lowered eyes, they moved past her. Anne-
Marie Stretter began to descend the stairs, and then he,
Michael Richardson. Lol's eyes followed them across
the garden. When she could no longer see them, she
slumped to the floor, unconscious.

Lol, Madame Stein relates, was taken home to South Tahla, and remained in her room, without once leaving it, for several weeks.

Her story, as well as that of Michael Richardson, became a subject of common gossip.

During this period, they say, Lol's collapse was marked by signs of suffering. But what is one to make of suffering which has no apparent cause?

She kept on repeating the same things: that it wasn't late, it was only summer that made it seem so.

She uttered her own name with anger: Lol Stein— she always referred to herself by her full name.

Then, more explicitly, she complained of being unbearably tired of waiting that way. She was bored, so bored she wanted to scream. And, in fact, she did scream that she had nothing to think about while she was waiting, she demanded, with childlike impatience, an immediate remedy for this deficiency. Yet none of the distractions that had been offered her had in any way affected this condition.

Then Lol stopped complaining altogether. Little by little, she even stopped talking. Her anger waned, grew discouraged. The only times she did speak was to say how impossible it was for her to express how boring and long it was, how interminable it was, to be Lol Stein. They asked her to try and pull herself together. She didn't understand why she should, she said. The difficulty she experienced in searching for a single word seemed insurmountable. She acted as though she expected nothing further from life.

Was she thinking of something, of herself? they asked her. She didn't understand the question. It seemed as though she took everything for granted, and that the infinite weariness of being unable to escape from the state she was in was not something that had to be thought about, that she had become a desert into which some nomad-like faculty had propelled her, in the interminable search for what? They did not know. Nor did she offer any answer.

Lol's collapse, her state of depression, her immense

suffering—time alone would be the healer, they kept saying. Her collapse was judged to be less serious than her initial delirium, it was not expected to last very long or result in any basic change in Lol's psychic constitution. Her extreme youth would soon bring her out of it. Her condition was easily explainable: Lol was suffering from a temporary inferiority complex for the simple reason that she had been jilted by the man from Town Beach. She was presently paying—it was bound to happen sooner or later—the price for the strange absence of pain she had experienced during the ball itself.

Then, although she still remained aloof and uncommunicative, she again began to ask for something to eat, for the window to be opened, to be allowed to sleep. And before long she began to enjoy having someone beside her to talk to her. She agreed with everything that was said and related in her presence, with every assertion made. To her, every remark was of equal importance. She was an avid listener.

She never asked for any news of them. She posed no questions. And when they thought it necessary to apprise her of their separation—she only learned later of his departure—the calm way she reacted was taken as a good sign. Her love for Michael Richardson was dying. There could be no question about it, it had been with a part of her recently-recovered reason that she had learned this news, this rightful reversal of events, this rightful retribution which was her due.

The first time she went out was at night, alone and without telling anyone she was going.

John Bedford was walking on the sidewalk. He was

about a hundred yards from her—she had just that moment come out—in front of her family's house. When she saw him, she hid behind the gatepost.

John Bedford's account of that night's events, as told to Lol herself, contributes, it seems to me, to her recent history. They are the last clear facts. After which, they fade almost completely from this story for ten years.

John Bedford did not see her leave the house, he took her to be some girl out walking, someone who was frightened by him, a man alone, so late at night. The boulevard was deserted.

Her silhouette was young, lissome, and when he came abreast of the gate he looked in.

What caught his attention was her smile, an apprehensive smile, admittedly, but none the less clearly overjoyed at seeing this chance stroller, him, coming by that evening.

He stopped and returned her smile. She emerged from her hiding place and came toward him.

Nothing in her manner or way of dress gave any hint of her condition, except perhaps her hair, which was in disarray. But it was possible that she might have been running, and there was a bit of wind that night. It was entirely possible that she had run to this spot from the other end of the deserted boulevard, thought John Bedford, for the simple reason that she had been frightened.

"I can walk with you, if you're afraid."

She did not answer. Nor did he press her. He began to walk on, and she started walking beside him, with obvious pleasure, almost sauntering.

It was when they reached the end of the boulevard,

out where the suburbs began, that John Bedford first realized that she was not headed anywhere in particular.

This intrigued John Bedford no end. Of course the idea of insanity occurred to him, but he dismissed it. As he dismissed the notion of an amorous adventure. She was doubtless playing some game. She was very young.

"Which way are you going?"

She tried to concentrate, glanced back down the boulevard, from where they had just come, but did not point back in that direction.

"Well . . ." she said.

He burst out laughing, and she laughed with him, wholeheartedly.

"Come on, let's go in this direction."

Meekly, she went back the way they had come, following him.

Still, he was more and more intrigued by her silence. Because it was coupled with an extraordinary curiosity about the places they were passing, no matter how completely ordinary they might be. It was as though she had not only just arrived in town, but that she had come there for the specific purpose of looking for or discovering something—a house, a garden, a street, even some object which, presumably, was extremely important to her, something she could find only at night.

"I live not far from here," said John Bedford. "If you're looking for something, perhaps I can help you."

She answered distinctly:

"I'm not."

Whenever he stopped, she stopped too. He amused himself by testing her. But she failed to notice the game he was playing. He continued walking. Once he stopped for a considerable length of time: she waited for him. John Bedford gave up the game. He let her do as she pleased. While seeming to lead the way, he followed her.

He noticed that by being extremely careful, by pretending to follow her every time they turned a corner, her momentum carried her along, she kept on walking forward, but no more or no less purposefully than the wind which sweeps into whatever nooks and crannies it chances to find.

He made her walk a little longer, then it occurred to him, in order to see what her reaction would be, to come back to the boulevard, to the spot where he had found her. She stiffened visibly as they passed a certain house. He recognized the gate behind which she had hidden. The house was large. The front door was still open.

It was at this point that it struck him that she might be Lol Stein. He did not know the Stein family, but he knew that she lived somewhere in that part of town. Like all the solid, middle-class citizens in town, most of whom spent their vacations in Town Beach, he knew what had happened to the girl.

He stopped, took her hand. She did not resist. He kissed the hand, there was a stale odor about it, an odor of dust, on her ring finger was an extremely beautiful engagement ring. The newspapers had already carried the story of wealthy Michael Richardson's liquidation of his land holdings, and of his departure for Calcutta.

The ring exploded in a dazzle of light. Lol looked at it, yes, she too looked at it in the same curious way she looked at everything else.

"You're Miss Stein, aren't you?"

She nodded several times, uncertainly at first, then with more and more assurance.

"Yes."

Still meekly, she followed him home.

There she lapsed into a state of happy nonchalance. He talked to her. He told her that he was an executive in an airplane factory, that he was an avid amateur musician, that he had just come back from a vacation in France. She listened to him talk. He said that he was happy to have met her.

"What do you want?"

In spite of a visible effort, she could not manage a reply. He let the matter drop.

Her hair had the same odor as her hand, the odor of some long-unused object. She was beautiful, but there was a sadness about her, as though the blood were slow to circulate in her veins, a grayish pallor. Her features were already beginning to fade into that pallor, to bury themselves anew in the depths of her flesh. She had grown younger. She looked no more than fifteen. Even when I met her later, she still had that morbidly young look about her.

She wrenched her eyes away from the intensity of his gaze and, with an imploring whimper, said:

"I have plenty of time, oh, how long it is!"

She raised herself toward him, someone suffocating, coming up for air, and he kissed her. That was what she wanted. She gripped him tightly and returned his kiss, kissed him hard enough to hurt him, as if she loved him, this total stranger. He said to her, and his voice was kindly:

"Maybe you two can start all over again."

He liked her. She aroused in him his special penchant for young girls, girls not completely grown into adults, for pensive, impertinent, inarticulate young girls. He broke the news to her without meaning to:

"Perhaps he'll come back."

She groped for words, said slowly:

"Who's gone away?"

"Didn't you know? Michael Richardson sold off all his real estate. He's gone to India, to join Mrs. Stretter."

She shook her head the way people often do, a trifle sadly.

"You know," he said, "I didn't blame them the way most people did."

He excused himself, saying he was going to call her mother. She made no effort to stop him.

Her mother, after she had received John Bedford's call, arrived a second time to bring her daughter home. It was the last time. This time Lol followed her, as a few moments before she had followed John Bedford.

John Bedford asked for her hand in marriage without ever having laid eyes on her again.

Their story soon became common knowledge—South Tahla was not large enough to remain silent about and absorb such an adventure—and of John Bedford it was said that he was capable of loving only women whose hearts had been broken and, what was more serious, that he had a strange penchant for young girls who had been jilted, and driven mad, by someone else.

Lol's mother informed her of the peculiar offer made by the chance stranger. Did she remember him? Yes, she did remember him. She accepted. John Bedford, her mother told her, would be obliged to move away from South Tahla for several years, because of his work. Would she agree to that too? She agreed to that too.

One day in October Lol Stein found herself married to John Bedford.

The wedding was not a strictly private affair, for Lol was much better, so it was said, and her parents wished, insofar as it was possible, to make her forget her earlier engagement. They took the precaution, however, of not inviting any of Lol's former friends, not even her best girlfriend Tatiana Karl. This precaution actually backfired. It only lent substance to the belief, held to by some, including Tatiana Karl, that Lol was a deeply disturbed girl.

Lol Stein was thus married, without wanting to be, in the way that she wished, without her having to resort to the grotesque incongruity of a choice, or to repeat, in what, in the eyes of some people, would have amounted to a kind of plagiarism, the crime of replacing the man from Town Beach who had just jilted her with some unique person of her own choice, and above all without having betrayed the exemplary abandon in which he had left her.

Lol moved away from South Tahla, the town where she had been born, and went to live in the town of Uxbridge, where she remained for ten years.

During the years that followed her marriage she had three children.

For ten years, it was thought by everyone around her, she was faithful to John Bedford. Whether or not this term had any meaning whatsoever for her is doubtless something we will never know. The two of them never once discussed either Lol's past or that extraordinary night at Town Beach.

Even after she was better she was never interested in learning what had become of the people she had known prior to her marriage. The death of her mother —Lol had wished to see her as seldom as possible after her marriage—left her dry-eyed. But this indifference of Lol's was never a subject of serious concern to those around her. They discounted it by saying that she had grown that way from having suffered so terribly. She, once so tender—they said that as they talked about everything else relating to her past, which had now become dead coals—had naturally grown somewhat hard, and even a trifle unjust, since her unhappy love affair with Michael Richardson. They found excuses for her, especially when her mother died.

She seemed confident about her future, appeared to have little desire to modify it. When she was with her husband, it was said, she was relaxed, and even happy. Sometimes she accompanied him on his business trips. She went to his concerts, urged him to continue with his music, encouraged him in fact to do anything his heart desired, not excluding, it was also said, being unfaithful to her with some of the younger girls who worked in his factory.

John Bedford claimed that he loved his wife. He said that he loved her still, the way she was, the way she had always been, both before and since their marriage, that he did not believe he had changed her so much as chosen her wisely and well. He loved this woman, this

Lola Valerie Stein, this calm presence by his side, this sleeping beauty who never offered a word of complaint, this upright sleeping beauty, this constant self-effacement which kept him moving back and forth between the forgetfulness and the rediscovery of her blondness, of this silken body which no awakening would ever change, of this constant, silent promise of something different which he called her gentleness, the gentleness of his wife.

Lol's home was a model of neatness. This obsessive orderliness, both in space and in time, was more or less of the kind she desired, not quite but almost. The schedule she set for their daily routine was rigorously adhered to. And likewise everything in the house had its proper place. It would have been impossible, everyone around Lol agreed, to come any closer to perfection.

Sometimes, especially when Lol was not at home, John Bedford must have been struck by this impeccable order. By this taste, too, this cold, ready-made taste. The decoration and furnishing of the bedrooms and living room were the faithful facsimile of model rooms displayed in store windows, and Lol's garden was the replica of all the other gardens in Uxbridge. Lol was imitating someone, but who? the others, all the others, as many people as possible. On afternoons when she was not there, didn't her house become the empty stage upon which was performed the soliloquy of some absolute passion whose meaning remained unrevealed? And wasn't it inevitable that John Bedford was sometimes afraid of it? That it was here that he had to be on the lookout for the first sign of thaw, of the winter ice breaking? Who knows? Who knows if he heard it one day?

But it takes very little to reassure John Bedford, and when his wife was present—which was most of the time —when she presided over her kingdom, it tended to lose its aggressive quality, was less prone to raise disturbing questions. Lol made her order seem almost natural; it suited her perfectly.

Ten years of marriage passed.   *not imp. to J.H.*

One day John Bedford was offered a choice of several better positions in various towns, one of which was South Tahla. He had always slightly regretted having moved away from South Tahla after his marriage, which he had done at the behest of Lol's mother.

Ten years had also gone by since Michael Richardson's departure. And not only had Lol never once alluded to it, as she grew older she seemed to become increasingly happy. Thus, if John Bedford had a moment's hesitation about accepting the offer, it was not difficult for Lol to persuade him otherwise. She merely said that she would be most happy to move back into her parents' house, which till then had been rented out.

John Bedford respected her wishes.

Lol Stein furnished and arranged her own house in South Tahla with the same impeccable care as she had the one in Uxbridge. She managed to instill in the new house the same icy order, to run it according to the same clocklike schedule. The furniture was the same. She worked very hard on the garden, which had been allowed to go to seed, she had already devoted considerable time to the earlier garden in Uxbridge, but this time, as she was laying out the pathways, she made a mistake. She wanted the garden paths to fan out evenly around the porch. But none of them intersected, and as a result they were unusable. John Bedford was much amused by the error. They laid out other, lateral paths which intersected the first ones and made walking a practical possibility.

Since her husband's position was a much better one than before, Lol, at South Tahla, hired a governess and was thus relieved for the first time of the full responsibility of the children.

She had some free time, a great deal of free time all of a sudden, and she got into the habit of taking walks through this town where she had grown up, and through the surrounding areas.

While at Uxbridge Lol had rarely gone out, so seldom in fact that her husband had sometimes forced her to go out for the sake of her health, here in South Tahla she took up the habit on her own.

At first she went out only when she needed to do some shopping. Then she went out without any pretext whatever, regularly, every day.

Within a very short time these walks became indispensable to her, as everything else she had done had previously been: punctuality, order, sleep.

To level the terrain, to dig down into it, to open the tombs wherein Lol is feigning death, seems to me fairer—given the necessity to fill in the missing links of Lol Stein's story—than to fabricate mountains, create obstacles, rely on chance. And, knowing this woman, I believe she would prefer that I compensate in this way for the lack of cold, hard facts about her life.

Moreover, in doing so I am always relying on hypotheses which are in no way gratuitous but which, in my opinion, have at least some slight foundation in fact.

Thus, even though Lol never said a word to anyone about what follows, the governess does remember it vaguely: the calm of the street on certain days, the occasional passage of lovers strolling by arm-in-arm, the way Lol shied away—the woman had been working at the Bedfords only for a short time and had never before seen her act this way. And since I, for my part, seem also to remember something, let me go on:

After she was settled in her house—there remained only one more bedroom on the second floor to furnish—one afternoon on a gray day a woman had passed Lol's house, and Lol had noticed her. The woman was not alone. The man with her had turned and looked at the freshly painted house and the neat grounds in which the gardeners were working. As soon as Lol had seen the couple turn into the street she had hidden behind a hedge, and they had not seen her. The woman had also looked up at the house, but less pointedly than the man, as though she were already familiar with it. They had exchanged a few words which, in spite of the quiet street, Lol had not been able to catch, except for the isolated phrase, spoken by the woman:

"Dead maybe."

After they had passed the Bedfords' grounds they had stopped. He had taken the woman in his arms and, furtively, had kissed her long and passionately. The sound of a car had caused him to let her go. They had parted. The man went back up the street the way he had come, walking quickly now, and had passed the house without so much as glancing at it this time.

In her garden, Lol is not certain that she has recognized the woman. There was something vaguely familiar about her face. About her way of walking, about her look too. But does the guilty, the delightful kiss they have exchanged in parting, the kiss Lol had chanced to see, does that kiss not also awaken something in her memory?

She does not dwell any further on who it was she had seen or not seen. She waits.

It is not long after this that she finds some excuse—she who never needed any excuse for anything—for going out walking through the streets.

As for the connection between these excursions and the passage of the couple, I see it less in the glimmer of recognition Lol had for the woman she had happened to see than in the words that the woman had let slip in an offhand way and that, in all probability, Lol had heard.

Lol stirred, she turned over in her sleep. Lol went out for walks through the streets, she learned to walk without having any special goal in mind.

Once out of the house, the moment she reached the street, the moment she began to walk, her walk absorbed her completely, delivered her from the desire to be or to do anything, even more than the immobility of dreams had up to that point. The streets bore Lol Stein along during her walks, that I know.

On several occasions I followed her without her ever realizing I was there, without her ever looking back, caught up as she was by something directly ahead of her.

Some insignificant accident, which she probably would not even have been able to remember, determined the circuitous route she took: the emptiness of a street, the way another curved, some dress shop displaying the latest fashions, the rectilinear bleakness of some boulevard, love, couples locked in close embrace in the remote corners of some public park or under the archways of streetside doors. At such times she passed by in a religious silence. Sometimes she took the lovers by surprise—they never noticed her coming—and startled them. She no doubt excused herself, but in a voice so low that in all likelihood no one ever heard her apologies.

The center of South Tahla is sprawling and modern, with broad perpendicular streets. The residential section is located to the west of this center, covers a considerable area, and is full of meandering streets and unexpected dead ends. Beyond this section lie a forest and fields, and a network of highways. Lol has never ventured as far as the forest on that side of South Tahla. She has explored the other side of town in great detail, the side where her house is located, hemmed in by the large industrial suburb.

South Tahla is a fairly large town, large enough so that Lol was reasonably certain that she could pass unperceived when she went on her walks. All the more so because there was no one section she preferred, she walked through all of them and seldom returned to the same places.

Nothing, moreover, about Lol's clothing or conduct

was such as to attract any special attention. The only thing that might have was her personage itself, Lola Stein, the girl jilted at the Town Beach casino years ago, who had been born and raised in South Tahla. But assuming there were some people who might have recognized her as this girl, the victim of Michael Richardson's monstrous, despicable behavior, who would ever have been tactless or spiteful enough to remind her of it? Who would have said:

"Pardon me, Miss, but if I'm not mistaken, aren't you Lola Stein?"

No one.

Though it had been rumored in town that the Bedfords had moved back to South Tahla, and though some people had been able to confirm the rumor, having seen the young woman pass by, no one had tried to talk to her. They no doubt decided that she had taken a big step in coming back, and that she deserved to be left alone.

I do not think it ever occurred to Lol that people went out of their way to avoid greeting her in order not to put her in the embarrassing situation of reminding her of a painful experience out of the past, of some difficult moment from her former life, since she herself did not take the initiative of greeting anyone and thus seemed to indicate her wish to forget.

No, Lol must have given herself the credit for passing unperceived in South Tahla, she must have considered it a test she had to pass every day and from which she daily emerged victorious. Each day, following her walk, she must have felt all the more reassured: if she willed it, people scarcely saw her, she was almost invisible. She thought that she had been cast into a mold, the identity of which was extremely vague and to which a variety of names might be given, an identity whose visibility she could control.

The couple's definitive move back to South Tahla, its stability, its handsome home, its relative wealth, its children, the quiet regularity of Lol's walks, the tasteful sobriety of her gray coat, the fashionable cut of her dark dresses—did not all these things attest to the fact that she had emerged forever from a traumatic experience? I can't say for sure. But one fact is certain: no one went up and tried to talk to her during those weeks when she went wandering happily through the town, no one.

And what about her, did she, Lol, recognize anyone in South Tahla? Aside from the woman—and she was not even sure about her—she had glimpsed that overcast day in front of her house? I doubt it.

When I followed her—from a concealed vantage point across the street—I could see that she sometimes smiled at certain faces, or at least that was the impression one got. But Lol's captive submissive smile, the immutable smugness of her smile, was such that people never did any more than smile in turn. She seemed to be mocking both herself and the other person, a trifle embarrassed but also amused at finding herself on the other side of the wide river which separated her from the people of South Tahla, the side they were not on.

Thus Lol Stein found herself back in South Tahla again, the town where she had been born, that town she knew like the back of her hand, without having anything, no visible sign by which she could tell that she had been recognized in return. She recognized South Tahla, recognized it constantly both from having known it earlier in her life and from having known it the evening before, but without there being any proof reflected by South Tahla to reinforce her own, each time that she recognized something, a bullet whose impact was always the same. All by herself, she began to recognize less, and then, in a different way, she began to return day after day, step by step, toward her non-knowledge of South Tahla.

This one place in the world where, it was thought, she had, in time past, lived through a painful experience, or what they called a painful experience, is by slow degrees erased from the very fiber of her memory. Why these rather than other places? No matter where she is, it is as though Lol is there for the first time. She no longer experiences the invariable distance that memory provides: she is there, in the present. Her presence renders the town pure, unrecognizable. She begins to walk in the sumptuous palace of South Tahla's oblivion.

When she returned home—John Bedford admitted this fact to Tatiana Karl—and resumed her place in the midst of the order she had created, she was happy, as fresh as when she had got up in the morning, was more relaxed with the children and more inclined to let them have their own way, even going so far as to take their side against the servants, in order to make them more independent of her, and to cover up their mistakes; when they were insolent to her, she forgave them, as always; slight delays and deviations from her fixed routine, which in the morning would have irritated her no end, passed virtually unnoticed after she had returned from her walks. Moreover, she began to discuss this order with her husband.

She told him one day that he might be right, that this methodical order was perhaps not what was needed—why she didn't say—and that she might change her ways sometime in the near future. When? Sometime later. Lol left it vague.

She used to say every day, as though she were saying it for the first time, that she had gone for a walk to such and such a place, and mention the section of town, but she never described the slightest incident she might have witnessed. John Bedford found his wife's lack of candor about her walks perfectly natural, especially since she was reserved about everything she did, about all her activities. It was rare for her to offer an opinion, never once did she relate a story or incident. But did not Lol's contentment, which seemed constantly greater, prove that she found nothing bitter or sad about the town of her youth? That was all that mattered, John Bedford must have thought.

Lol never mentioned any purchases she might have made. Nor, in fact, did she ever make any during her walks in South Tahla. Nor did she ever so much as comment on the weather.

When it was raining, those around her knew that Lol would watch from the windows of her room to spot any sign of the weather's clearing. I suspect that it was there, in the monotony of the rain, that she found that "elsewhere," that uniform, insipid, and sublime "elsewhere" which she cherished more than any other moment in her present existence, that "elsewhere" she had been looking for since her return to South Tahla.

She devoted her entire morning to her household, her children, to the observance of that strict order which she alone had the strength and ability to impose, but when it rained too hard for her to go out, she did absolutely nothing. This domestic fervor—she tried to conceal it as best she could—vanished completely when it came time for her to go out, or when she decided to go out even if she had had a particularly difficult morning.

How had she spent these same hours during the ten preceding years? I asked her that question. She really didn't know what to reply. At Uxbridge, had she spent these same hours doing nothing? Nothing. And that was all? She didn't know how to express it: nothing. Behind the windows? Perhaps that too, yes. But then again . . .

Here is my opinion:

Thoughts, a welter of thoughts, all rendered equally sterile the moment her walk was over—none of these thoughts had ever crossed the threshold with her into her house—occur to Lol as she walks. It would seem as though it was the mechanical movement of her body which summoned them forth, all of them together, in a chaotic, confused, and ample surge. Lol receives them with pleasure, and with constant amazement. Some fresh air slips into her house, disturbs her, and drives her from it. Then the thoughts begin to come.

Thoughts born and reborn, daily, always the same thoughts that come crowding in, come to life and breathe, in an accessible, boundless universe, out of which one thought, and only one, eventually manages at long last to make itself heard, become visible, slightly more visible than the others, pressuring Lol, somewhat more insistently than the others, to retain it.

In the distance the ball trembles, ancient, the only wreck on a now-peaceful ocean, in the rain at South Tahla. Tatiana, when I later mentioned this to her, shared my opinion.

"So that was why she took those walks, to have a chance to think more clearly about the ball."

The ball revives, ever so slightly, shimmers, clings to Lol. She gives it warmth, protects it, nourishes it, and it grows, ventures forth from the protective layers, stretches, and one day is ready.

She enters it.

She enters it every day.

That summer, Lol fails to see the light of the afternoon. No, she is making her way into the wondrous, artificial light of the Town Beach ball. And in this enclosure, that opens wide to her eyes alone, she begins again to live in the past, she arranges it, puts order into the dwelling place that is truly hers.

"A real masochist," says Tatiana, "she must constantly be thinking about the same thing."

I agree with Tatiana.

I know Lol Stein in the only way I can; through love. It is because of this knowledge that I have come to this conclusion: among the many aspects of the Town Beach ball, what fascinates Lol is the end. It is the precise moment when it comes to an end, when dawn arrives with incredible cruelty and separates her from the couple formed by Michael Richardson and Anne-Marie Stretter, forever, forever. Each day Lol goes ahead with the task of reconstructing that moment. She even manages to seize a little of its lightning-like rapidity, to spread it out and pinpoint each second, arrest its movement, an immobility which is extremely precarious but, for her, infinitely graceful.

Again she goes out walking. She sees more and more clearly, precisely, what she wants to see. What she is reconstructing is the end of the world.

She sees herself—and this is what she really believes —in the same place, at the end, always, in the center of a triangular construction of which dawn, and the two of them, are the eternal sides: it is the moment when she has just become aware of that dawn, while they have not yet noticed it. She knows; they still do not. She is powerless to prevent them from knowing. And it begins all over again:

At that precise moment, some attempt—but what?— should have been made which was not. At that precise moment Lol is standing, completely undone, with no voice to cry out for help, with no convincing argument, with no proof of how unimportant the coming day was compared to that night, uprooted and borne from dawn toward that couple, her whole being filled with a chronic, hopeless feeling of panic. She is not God, she is no one.

She smiles, yes, she smiles at that remembered minute of her life. The naiveté of some eventual suffering, or even of some commonplace sadness, no longer plays a part in it. All that remains of that minute is time in all its purity, bone-white time.

And again it begins: the windows closed, sealed, the ball immured in its nocturnal light, would have contained all three of them, and they alone. Lol is positive of that: together they would have been saved from the advent of another day, of one more day at least.

What would have happened? Lol does not probe very deeply into the unknown into which this moment opens. She has no memory, not even an imaginary one, she has not the faintest notion of this unknown. But what she does believe is that she must enter it, that that was what she had to do, that it would always have meant, for her mind as well as her body, both their greatest pain and their greatest joy, so commingled as to be undefinable, a single entity but unnamable for lack of a word. I like to believe—since I love her—that if Lol is silent in her daily life it is because, for a split second, she believed that this word might exist. Since it does not, she remains silent. It would have been an absence-word, a hole-word, whose center would have been hollowed out into a hole, the kind of hole in which all other words would have been buried. It would have been impossible to utter it, but it would have been made to reverberate. Enormous, endless, an empty gong, it would have held back anyone who had wanted to leave, it would have convinced them of the impossible, it would have made them deaf to any other word save that one, in one fell swoop it would have defined the future and the moment themselves. By its absence, this word ruins all the others, it contaminates them, it is also the dead dog on the beach at high noon, this hole of flesh. How were other words found? Hand-me-downs from God knows how many love affairs like Lol

Stein's, affairs nipped in the bud, trampled upon, and from massacres, oh! you've no idea how many there are, how many blood-stained failures are strewn along the horizon, piled up there, and, among them, this word, which does not exist, is none the less there: it awaits you just around the corner of language, it defies you—never having been used—to raise it, to make it arise from its kingdom, which is pierced on every side and through which flows the sea, the sand, the eternity of the ball in the cinema of Lol Stein.

They had watched the violinists file past, and been surprised.

What Lol would have liked would have been to have the ball immured, to make of it this ship of light upon which, each afternoon, she embarks, but which remains there, in this impossible port, forever anchored and yet ready to sail away with its three passengers from this entire future in which Lol Stein now takes her place. There are times when it has, in Lol's eyes, the same momentum as on the first day, the same fabulous force.

But Lol is not yet God, nor anyone.

He would have divested her slowly of her black dress, and by the time he had done it a good part of the voyage would have been over.

I saw Lol undress herself, still inconsolable, inconsolable.

For Lol, it is unthinkable that she not be present at the place where this gesture occurred. This gesture would not have occurred without her: she is with it flesh to flesh, form to form, her eyes riveted on its corpse. She was born to witness it. Others are born to

die. Without her to witness it, this gesture will die of
thirst, will disintegrate, fall, Lol is in ashes.

The tall, thin body of the other woman would have
appeared little by little. And, in a strictly parallel and
reverse progression, Lol would have been replaced by
her in the affection of the man from Town Beach. Replaced by that woman, unto her very breath. Lol holds
her breath as this woman's body appears to this man,
her own fades, fades, voluptuous pleasure, from the
world.

"You. You alone."

Lol had never been able to carry this divesting of
Anne-Marie Stretter's dress in slow-motion, this velvet
annihilation of her own person, to its conclusion.

I am of the opinion that Lol never thinks about
what happened between them after the ball, when she
was no longer there. The fact that he left forever, after
their separation, if she were to think about it, in spite
of herself, would remain a mark in his favor, would
only confirm the opinion that she had always had
about him that he could find true happiness only in
some short-lived and hopeless love, with courage, and
nothing more. Michael Richardson, in his time, had
been loved too deeply and completely; it was as simple
as that.

Lol no longer thinks of that love. It is dead, even has
the odor of dead love.

The man from Town Beach has only one task left to
accomplish, which is always the same in Lol's universe:
every afternoon, Michael Richardson begins to undress
a woman other than Lol, and when other breasts appear, white beneath the black sheath, he remains there

transfixed, a God wearied by this divesting, his only task, and in vain Lol waits for him to take her again, with her body rendered infirm by the other she cries out, she waits in vain, she cries out in vain.

Then one day this infirm body stirs in the womb of God.

The moment Lol saw him she recognized him. It was the man who had passed her house a few weeks before.

That day he was alone.

He was coming out of a cinema in the center of town. While the rest of the crowd hurried down the aisle, he took his time coming out. When he reached the sidewalk he blinked his eyes in the light, paused to

look around, did not see Lol Stein, he was carrying his
suitcoat with one hand, the coat slung over his shoulder, and with a movement of his arm he swung it back
around in front, tossed it lightly into the air, then
slipped it on, still taking his time.

Did he look like her fiancé from Town Beach? No,
not in the slightest. Did he have certain mannerisms
that reminded her of her dead lover? Yes, no doubt he
did, especially the way he looked at women. He too,
like the other one, must have been an incorrigible
ladies' man, must have borne the burdens of his body
only with them, this body which, with every glance,
demanded more. Yes, Lol decided, he did have, there
emanated from him, that initial expression that Michael Richardson had had, the one that Lol had known
before the ball.

He was not as young as Lol had thought the first
time she had seen him. But she may have been mistaken. She doubtless found that he must be an impatient person, perhaps easily given to cruelty.

He scanned the boulevard in the vicinity of the
cinema. Lol had taken refuge back around the corner
of the building.

Behind him, in her gray coat, Lol, unmoving, waits
for him to make up his mind which way to go.

This is what I see:

The heat of a summer which till that day she had
listlessly endured explodes and spreads. She is sub-
merged in it. Everything is: the street, the town, this
stranger. What heat, and what is this weariness? Nor is
it the first time she has felt it. For several weeks she has
sometimes wished she had a bed, or something akin to

a bed, right there where she was, a bed on which to lay this heavy, leaden body, this body so difficult to move, this thankless and tender maturity, just on the verge of falling down upon an unresponsive, all-devouring earth. Ah, what is this body with which she suddenly feels herself saddled? Whatever became of the indefatigable, birdlike body that had been hers up till now?

He made up his mind: he headed up the boulevard. Did he have a moment's hesitation? Yes. He looked at his watch and decided on that direction. Did Lol already know the name of the woman he was going to meet? Not yet, not quite. She is still unaware that it is the woman she has followed, through this man from South Tahla. And yet this woman is now no longer merely the woman she caught a glimpse of in front of her garden: I think she is already more for Lol.

If there was a certain place where he had to be at a certain time, he apparently had plenty of time between that and the present moment. He therefore spent it in the following manner, walking rather in that direction than in some other, in the vague hope, which he never abandoned, thought Lol, of meeting some other woman, of following her and standing up the one he was supposed to meet. He spent this time in a way Lol found exquisite.

He walked at a steady pace, close to the shop windows. He is not the first who, for the past several weeks, has been walking this way. He would turn and stare at any woman who was beautiful and alone, sometimes he would stop and ogle them in a vulgar way. Each time he did, Lol gave a start, as though he had done it to her.

On a beach, in the full flush of her youth, she had

previously seen someone act like this, the way a lot of men in South Tahla acted. Does she suddenly remember having been a victim of it? Does it make her smile? In all probability these tentative advances can be counted among Lol's happy and tender memories. Now she sees their surreptitious stares directed at her, in an absolute equivalence. She, who does not see herself, is thus seen, in others. Therein lies the omnipotence of this substance whereof she is made, without any particular ties.

They are walking on a beach, for her. They don't know it. She has no trouble following him. He takes big steps, but his torso, carefully controlled, moves hardly at all. He didn't know it.

It was a weekday. There were few people about. It was just before the height of the holiday season.

I see this:

Careful, calculating, she walks a good distance behind him. When he stares at another woman, she lowers her head or averts her gaze. What little he can see perhaps—this gray coat, this black beret, nothing more—is not dangerous. When he pauses in front of a shop window, or anything else, she slows down so that she won't have to stop at the same time as he. If they were to see her—the men from South Tahla—Lol would turn and run away.

She wants to follow. Follow, then take by surprise, threaten to surprise. She has wanted to for some time. If she wants to be taken by surprise in her turn, she does not want it to happen before she has decided on it.

The boulevard rises gently toward a square which

they reach at the same time. From there three other boulevards head out toward the suburbs. This is the side of town the forest is on. Children's shouts.

He followed the one that leads farthest away from the forest: a straight avenue, only recently opened, on which the traffic is heavier than on the others, the fastest route out of town. He began to walk faster. It was getting late. The time he had left before his appointment, the time they both had left, both he and Lol, was growing shorter and shorter.

Thus he was spending this time in a way that, in Lol's eyes, was perfect: looking for something. He wasted it well, he walked and walked. Each one of his steps echoes in Lol, strikes, strikes true, in the same place, the nail of flesh. For the past several days, the past several weeks, the steps of the men of South Tahla have been striking the same way.

This I invent, I see:

The only times she feels the suffocating heat of summer are when he does something besides just walking, when he runs his fingers through his hair, when he lights a cigarette, and especially when he eyes a passing woman. At these times Lol doubts that she has the strength to keep on following him, while she continues to do so, to follow this man among all the men of South Tahla.

Lol knew where this highway led once it had passed the houses on the square, and when it had also passed the small commercial center detached from the town proper, consisting of a cinema and a few bars.

I invent:

At that distance, he can't even hear the sound of her footsteps on the sidewalk.

She is wearing the silent, low-heeled shoes she wears to go walking. Still, she takes an added precaution, she removes her beret.

When he stops on the square where the boulevard ends, she takes off her gray coat too. She is in navy blue, a woman he still doesn't see.

He paused beside a bus stop. There was a large crowd of people, many more than in town.

Then Lol walks clear around the square and takes up a position near the stop for buses leaving in the opposite direction.

The sun had already disappeared, and its rays were lighting the rooftops.

He lighted a cigarette, paced back and forth a few times the length of the bus stop. He glanced at his watch, saw that it was not quite time, and waited. Lol found that he was capable of looking around him in half a dozen directions at once.

There were women there, a crush of women waiting for the bus, women crossing the square, women passing by. Not one of them escaped his glance, Lol imagined, not one who might have suited his fancy or, if worst came to worst, someone else's fancy, why not? He eyed their dresses like a ferret, thought Lol, perfectly at his ease there in the crowd while waiting for this appointment of which he already had a foretaste there right under his nose, taking, imagining he was having for a few seconds each of the women, then rejecting them, mourning each and every loss, mourning one alone, the one who did not yet exist but who, if she did, would be capable of making him, at the last minute, stand up the woman among a thousand others who was about to come, come toward Lol Stein, the woman Lol was waiting for with him.

She did in fact arrive, she descended from a bus crowded with people on their way home from work.

The moment she heads toward him, with that very slow, very gentle, circular movement of her hips which makes her, at every step, the object of some secret, ceaseless, caressing self-flattery, as soon as Lol sees the black mass of dry, mistlike hair with the tiny, white, triangular face beneath, that face dominated completely by those very large, very bright eyes, gravely disturbed by their ineffable remorse at belonging to this adulterous body, Lol admits that she recognized Tatiana Karl. Then, and only then, she believes, the name that had been hovering on the edge of her consciousness for weeks was there: Tatiana Karl.

She was discreetly dressed in a casual black suit. But her hair was done with great care, there was a gray flower in it, she had pinned it up with gold combs, and she had gone to great lengths to fasten her fragile hairdo with a long, wide, black hair band which, where it passed close to her face, framed her bright eyes, made them look even larger, even more sorrowful, and this hair-do, which would have been destroyed by the slightest exposure to the wind, which, in fact, a mere look would undo, she must have—Lol is speculating now—she must have had to imprison in a dark hair net so that, at the proper moment, he would be the only one who could breach and destroy its admirable artificiality, one single movement of his hand would bathe her in its fallen tresses, that marvelous head of hair which, suddenly, Lol remembers and sees again, luminously juxtaposed to this one. In those days people said that, sooner or later, she would have to have her hair cut, that its sheer weight would wear her out and make her round-shouldered, would disfigure her because its mass was disproportionate to her large eyes and the tiny bone structure of her thin face. Tatiana Karl has not cut her hair, she has accepted the challenge of having too much.

Is that the way Tatiana looked that day? Or somewhat, or completely, different? There were times when she wore her hair down, in a long pony tail, times when she wore light-colored dresses. I no longer know for sure.

They exchanged a few words and started walking down that avenue, out beyond the suburbs.

They kept a step apart. They scarcely spoke.

I think I can see what Lol Stein must have seen:

There is an incredible contact between them, which does not stem from an intimate knowledge of each other but, on the contrary, from a disdain for such knowledge. They both have the same expression of silent consternation, of terror, of profound indifference. The closer they get to their destination, the faster they walk. Lol Stein watches these lovers, she devours them with her eyes, she invents them. She is not deceived by the way they look, not she. They don't love each other. What is there for her to say? Others surely would say it. If she were to talk she would phrase it differently, but she does not speak. Other ties bind them in a grip which is not one of sentiment or of happiness, it is something else which bestows neither joy nor sorrow. They are neither happy nor unhappy. Their union is constructed upon indifference, in a way which is general and which they apprehend moment by moment, a union from which all preference is excluded. They are together, two trains which meet and pass, around them the landscape, sensuous and lushly green, is the same, they see it, they are not alone. One can come to terms with them. By opposite paths, they have arrived at the same result as Lol Stein, they by doing, saying, by trying and failing, by going away and coming back, by lying, losing, winning, advancing, by coming back again, and she, Lol, by doing nothing.

There is a choice seat waiting to be taken, a seat which she failed to have ten years before in Town Beach. But where? It can't be compared to that opera seat in Town Beach. But what seat is it then? She will have to be content with this one so that, at last, she can make her way, move a step or two toward that distant bank upon which they, the others, dwell. Toward what? What is that bank?

The long, narrow building must have been used sometime in the past either as a barracks or as some kind of administration building. One section of it serves as a garage for buses. The other is the Forest Hotel, of doubtful reputation but the only place in town where couples can meet in complete confidence. The street it faces is called Forest Boulevard, and the hotel is the last number on the street. Along its façade stands a row of ancient alder trees, some of which are missing. Behind the hotel there stretches a broad field of rye, smooth and treeless.

There is still a last vestige of sunlight on this flat landscape, on this field.

Lol remembers this hotel from the times she went there as a young girl with Michael Richardson. And she has probably ventured out as far as this hotel on some of her walks. It was there that Michael Richardson told her he loved her. The memory of that winter afternoon has, like the rest, been engulfed in forgetfulness, been swallowed up in the slow, daily glaciation of South Tahla beneath her footsteps.

It was here, on this same spot, that a girl from South

Tahla began to adorn herself—it must have taken several months—for the Town Beach ball. It was from here that she left to go to that ball.

On Forest Boulevard, Lol slackens her step. There's no point in following so close behind now that she knows where they're going. The worst that could happen is that she might run the risk of being recognized by Tatiana Karl.

When she reaches the hotel, they have already gone upstairs.

Lol, on the street, waits. The sun is setting. Dusk is falling, in a rush of red, doubtless sad. Lol waits.

Lol Stein is behind the Forest Hotel, stationed at one corner of the building. Time passes. She has no idea whether the rooms that look out over the field of rye are still the ones they rent out by the hour. This field, only a few short yards from her, is plunged, deeper and deeper, into a green, milky shadow.

On the third floor of the Forest Hotel, a light goes on in one of the windows. Yes. They are the same rooms as in her day.

I see how she gets there. Very quickly, she reaches the field of rye, slips into it, sits down in it, stretches out in it. Before her is that lighted window. But Lol is far from its light.

The idea of what she is doing never crosses her mind. I still maintain that this is the first time, that she is there without the faintest idea of being there, that, if she were asked, she would simply say that she was resting. From the fatigue of getting there. From the fatigue that will follow. From the necessity of returning. Living, dying, she breathes deeply, tonight the air is like honey, cloyingly sweet. She does not even question the source of the wonderful weakness which has brought her to lie in this field. She lets it act upon her, fill her until she thinks she will suffocate, lets it lull her roughly, pitilessly, until Lol Stein is fast asleep.

The rye rustles beneath her loins. Young, early-summer rye. Her eyes riveted on the lighted window, a woman hearkens to the void—feeding upon, devouring this non-existent, invisible spectacle, the light from a room where others are.

In the distance, with fairy-like fingers, the recollection of a certain memory flits past. It grazes Lol not long after she has lain down in the field, it portrays for her, at this late evening hour in the field of rye, this woman who is gazing up at a small rectangular window, a narrow stage, circumscribed as a stone, on which no actor has yet appeared. And perhaps Lol is afraid, but ever so slightly, of the possibility of an even greater separation from the others. She is none the less fully aware that some people would struggle—yesterday she still would have—that they would go running home as fast as they could the moment some vestige of reason had made them discover themselves in this field. But this is the last fear Lol has learned, the fear that others might have in her place, that evening. They would bravely destroy it within themselves. But she, on the contrary, cherishes it, tames it, caresses it with her hands on the rye.

Beyond the other side of the hotel, the horizon has lost its last traces of color. Night is falling.

The shadow of the man crosses the rectangle of light.

Once, then a second time, back in the opposite direction.

The light changes, grows brighter. Now it is no longer coming from the back of the room, to the left of the window, but from the ceiling.

In turn, Tatiana Karl, naked in her black hair, crosses the stage of light, slowly. It is perhaps in Lol's rectangle of vision that she pauses. She turns back to the room where the man presumably is.

The window is small, and no doubt Lol can see only the upper part of the lovers' bodies, from the waist up. Thus it is that she cannot see the full length of Tatiana's tresses.

From this distance she cannot hear them when they talk. All she can see is their facial expressions—coinciding with the movements of parts of their bodies—which bespeak disenchantment. Their words are few. But then, she can only see them when they pass back and forth, in line with the window, at the back of the room. The mute expressions on their faces are also much alike, Lol finds.

Again he passes through the light, dressed this time. And not long after him, Tatiana Karl, still naked: she stops, stretches, her head slightly raised and, pivoting the upper part of her body, her arms in the air, her hands ready to receive it, she pulls her hair around in front of her, coils it, and puts it up. Compared to the slenderness of her body, her breasts are heavy, time has wrought its damaging effect upon them, the only part of her body which has so suffered. Lol must remember how pristine and lovely they once had been. Tatiana Karl is the same age as Lol Stein.

I remember: the man comes over while she is busy fixing her hair, he leans over and buries his head in the supple, abundant mass, kisses her, while she, still busy putting up her hair, acquiesces, neutral and indolent.

They disappear from the window for a fairly long time.

Then Tatiana comes back again alone, with her hair down once more. This time she goes to the window, a cigarette in her mouth, and leans out.

Lol, I can see Lol: she does not stir. She knows that, unless they had been forewarned of her presence in the field, they would never be able to detect her. Tatiana does not see the dark spot in the rye.

Tatiana moves away from the window, to reappear dressed once more in her black suit. He too goes by, one last time, his suitcoat slung over his shoulder.

A moment later, the light goes out in the room.

A taxi, probably summoned by phone, stops in front of the hotel.

Lol gets up. It is completely dark now. She is numb, at first she has trouble walking, but she sets off at a brisk pace. When she reaches the small square she finds a taxi. It's time for dinner. She is terribly late.

Her husband is outside in the street, waiting, beside himself with worry.

She lies, and is believed. She tells them that she had to go all the way to the outskirts of town to do an errand, something she could buy only in the nurseries in the suburbs, plants for a hedge she was thinking of putting in to help screen the grounds from the street.

They commiserated with her, told her how sorry

they were that she had had to walk so long and so far down dark, deserted streets.

The love that Lol had once had for Michael Richardson was her husband's best guarantee of his wife's faithfulness. It was impossible that she should ever find, a second time, a man made of the same cloth as the man from Town Beach, or, if she did, she would have to invent him, and she invented nothing, John Bedford believed.

During the days that followed, Lol looked high and low for Tatiana's address.

She did not give up her walks.

But the light of the ball was suddenly extinguished. She can no longer see it clearly. The faces, the bodies of the lovers are covered over with an even layer of gray mildew.

The Karls had never lived in South Tahla. It was at school that Lol and Tatiana had become fast friends, and they used to spend their vacations together in Town Beach. Their parents were barely acquainted. Lol had forgotten the Karls' address. She wrote to the alumnae association of the school: after Tatiana's father had retired, the family had moved away, they lived near the seashore now, not far from Town Beach. Since they had moved the association had lost track of Tatiana. Lol refused to admit defeat, she wrote a long, embarrassed letter to Mrs. Karl, telling her how much she would have liked to renew ties with Tatiana, the only friend she had not forgotten. Mrs. Karl wrote back a very affectionate letter and gave Lol the address of her daughter, who had been married for eight years to a Dr. Beugner, in South Tahla.

Tatiana was living in a large house in the southern part of South Tahla, not far from the forest.

On several occasions, Lol went out for walks in the vicinity of this house, with which she was already familiar, as she was familiar with all the houses in town.

The house was situated on a slight rise. The grounds, which were large and well-wooded, made it difficult to see the house from the front, but from behind, by looking up the winding vista of a broad pathway, it was more easily visible, with balconies on the upper stories and a large terrace where, in summer, Tatiana could often be found. It was here, in the rear, that the main gate was located.

It was probably not Lol's plan to rush over and call

on Tatiana, she no doubt planned first to scout out the area near her house, to loiter in the neighboring streets. Who could tell? Perhaps Tatiana would come out, they would meet in this way, run into each other again, to all appearances quite by chance.

That did not happen.

The first time, Lol must have seen Tatiana Karl on the terrace, lying on a deck chair, wearing a bathing suit, her eyes closed against the bright sunlight. The second time as well. Once, Tatiana Karl seemed not to be home. Her deck chair was there, and a coffee table covered with brightly colored magazines. That day the sky was overcast. Lol lingered in the neighborhood, but Tatiana failed to appear.

It was at that point that Lol made up her mind to call on Tatiana. She told her husband that she intended to go and see an old school friend, Tatiana Karl, whose picture she had happened to come across while she was straightening up some things. Had she ever spoken to him about her? She couldn't remember. No. It was the first time John Bedford had ever heard the name.

As Lol never expressed any desire to see anyone or look up anyone again, John Bedford was somewhat taken aback by this show of initiative. He questioned Lol. She stuck to the sole reason that she had given him: she was interested in catching up on the news of her old school friends, and especially this particular one, Tatiana Karl, who, as she recalled, was the most endearing of them all. How did she know her address in South Tahla? She had happened to see her come out of a cinema in the center of town, and had written to the alumnae association.

John Bedford had grown used to seeing his wife, all these years, fully contented with him alone, with no need of any outside contacts. The notion of Lol exchanging small talk with anyone, no matter who, was inconceivable, and even, apparently, somewhat distasteful, for anyone who really knew her. Still, it would appear that John Bedford did nothing to try and prevent Lol from finally acting the way other women did. It was something that had to happen sooner or later, and it confirmed how vastly improved she had grown over the years, it was something he had devoutly desired, John Bedford doubtless remembered, or, by then, did he really prefer that she remain the way she had been for ten years in Uxbridge, in that irreproachable promise of something different? I suspect that he had a moment of panic: what he had to be afraid of was himself. He had to pretend that he was pleased by Lol's initiative. He was delighted, he told her, by anything that would take her away from her daily routine. Didn't she realize that? And what about her walks? Would he have the pleasure of meeting Tatiana Karl? Lol promised that he would, sometime within the next few days.

Lol bought herself a dress. She put off her visit to Tatiana Karl for two days, the time it took her to make this difficult purchase. She decided on a white, summer dress. The dress, according to everyone in her house, suited her perfectly.

In secret, not allowing her husband or the children or the maids to see, she spent hours that day primping and preening. Her husband wasn't the only one, they all knew that she was going to pay a visit to an old school friend who had once been very close to her. They were surprised, but they carefully refrained from saying anything. When she was on the point of leaving the house, they complimented her on her appearance, and she felt obliged to offer certain additional information: she had chosen that white dress so that Tatiana Karl would be able to recognize her more readily, more easily. The last time she had seen Tatiana had been at the seashore in Town Beach, she could remember it very clearly, it was ten years ago, and during that vacation she had, at the request of a friend, worn nothing but white.

The deck chair was in its usual position, as were the table and the magazines. Tatiana Karl was perhaps in the house. It was a Saturday afternoon, about four o'clock. The sun was shining.

This is what I surmise:

Once again, Lol circles the house, no longer in the hope of running into Tatiana, but to try and control to some extent that impatience welling within her, impelling her to run: she must not give these people the slightest hint of her impatience, these people who are as yet unaware that their peace and tranquility is about to be shattered forever. In the course of the past few days, Tatiana Karl has become so dear to her that, if her attempt were to fail, if she were not able to see her again, the town would become unlivable, stifling and deadly. She had to succeed. For these people, the next few days are going to be—more specifically than a more distant future would be—whatever she cares to make of them, she, Lol Stein. She will invent the necessary circumstances, then she will open whatever doors have to be opened: they will pass through them.

She circles the house, until it is slightly past the time she has set for the visit.

In what lost universe has Lol Stein acquired this fierce will, this method?

Perhaps it would have been preferable for her to arrive at Tatiana's in the evening. But she has decided that she ought to show a certain discretion and abide by the customary visiting hours of the upper middle-class to which both she and Tatiana belong.

She rings the bell at the gate. It is as though she can feel the blood rising in her cheeks. Today she must be beautiful enough for it to be visible. Today, in keeping with her desire, they must see Lol Stein.

A maid came out onto the terrace, looked for a moment, and went back inside. A few seconds later, Tatiana, in a blue dress, appeared on the terrace in turn and looked.

The terrace is about a hundred yards from the gate. Tatiana is trying to make out who it is who has dropped in this way unannounced. She fails to discern who it is and gives the order to open the gate. Again the maid disappears. The gate opens with an electric click that startles Lol.

She is inside the fence, on the grounds. The gate closes behind her.

She advances up the path. She is half way up it when two men come out and join Tatiana. One of them is the man she is looking for. He sees her for the first time.

She smiles at the group and keeps on walking slowly toward the terrace. Flower beds come into view on the lawn, and on either side of the path hydrangeas are withering in the shade of the trees. They are already turning purple, is probably her only thought. The hydrangeas, Tatiana's hydrangeas, at the same time as Tatiana now, she who from one moment to the next is going to shout my name.

"Lola, is that really you?"

He looks at her. She discovers the same intrigued expression she had seen in the street. It really is Tatiana, here is Tatiana's voice, tender, suddenly tender, with its old modulations, her sad, childlike voice.

"But, is it Lol! I'm not mistaken?"

"It's Lol," she said.

Tatiana comes running down the terrace steps and over to Lol, stops before she reaches her, looks at her, her expression one of undisguised surprise but also slightly wild, changing from pleasure to displeasure, from fear to reassurance. Lol the intruder, the little girl in the playground, Lol from Town Beach, that ball, that ball, mad Lol, did she still love her? Yes.

Lol is in her arms.

On the terrace, the men watched them embrace. They have heard Tatiana speak of her.

They are almost at the terrace. At any moment, the distance separating them from that terrace is going to be covered, forever.

Before that happens, the man Lol is looking for suddenly finds himself in the direct line of her gaze. Lol, her head on Tatiana's shoulder, sees him: he almost lost his balance, he turned his head away. She was not mistaken.

Tatiana no longer has about her that fresh-linen smell of the dormitories where, in the evenings, her laughter used to ring out in search of a friendly ear to whom she could relate the practical jokes she had dreamed up for the next day. The next day is here. Tatiana, in her golden skin, smells of amber now, the present, the present alone, which turns round and round, whirls in the dust and at last alights with a cry, the soft cry with broken wings, and Lol is the only person to notice the break in it.

"Lord! It's been ten years since I've seen you, Lola!"

"Yes, ten years, Tatiana."

Arm in arm, they ascend the terrace steps. Tatiana introduces Peter Beugner, her husband, to Lol, and Jack Hold, a friend of theirs—the distance is covered —me.

I'm thirty-six years old, a member of the medical profession. I've been living in South Tahla only for a year. I'm in Peter Beugner's section at the State Hospital. I'm Tatiana Karl's lover.

From the moment Lol entered the house, she never so much as glanced at me again.

She immediately began talking to Tatiana about a photograph she had happened to come across while she was cleaning up a room in the attic recently: they were both in it, holding hands, in the school yard, dressed in the school uniform. They were fifteen. Tatiana didn't remember the picture. Personally, I believed it existed. Tatiana asked if she could see it. Lol promised to show it to her.

"Tatiana has talked to us about you," Peter Beugner said.

Tatiana isn't a very talkative person anyway, and that day she was even less so than usual. She hung on Lol Stein's every word, prodded her into talking about her recent life. She wanted both to acquaint us with, and learn more herself about, the way Lol lived, about her husband, her children, her house, how she spent her time, about her past: Lol was not the most talkative person in the world either, but she spoke clearly enough, rationally enough to reassure anyone who might have been concerned about her present condition—but not her, not Tatiana. No, Tatiana was concerned about Lol in a different way than were the others: that she had so completely recovered her sanity was a source of sadness to her. One should never be completely cured of one's passion. And besides, Lol's had been an ineffable passion, that she was quite willing to admit, even today, in spite of the reservations she still has concerning the part it had played in Lol's breakdown.

"You speak of your life as though you were reciting from a book," Tatiana said.

"From one year to the next," Lol said with a vague smile, "I see nothing any different around me."

"Tell me something, you know what I mean, about how we were when we were young," Tatiana begged.

Lol racked her brain, searching for something, some detail out of her youth that might have enabled Tatiana to rediscover some vestige of that real friendship she had felt for Lol during their school years together. She found nothing. She said:

"If you want my opinion, I think people were wrong in their judgment."

Tatiana did not reply.

The conversation drifted into platitudes, slowed, became dull because Tatiana was watching Lol like a hawk, waching her slightest smile, her every move, and that occupied her entirely. Peter Beugner spoke to Lol about South Tahla, and about the changes that had taken place in the town since the women had been young. Lol had followed each detail of South Tahla's development, the construction of new streets, the plans for new buildings in the suburbs, she spoke of it as she spoke of her life, in a calm, controlled voice. Then again silence set in. They talked of Uxbridge. They talked.

Nothing about this woman betrayed the slightest hint, even fleetingly, of Lol Stein's breakdown, her strange mourning for Michael Richardson.

Of her insanity—which had been eradicated, leveled —nothing seemed to remain, no trace except her presence that afternoon at Tatiana Karl's. The reason for her presence was a streak of color on a smooth, unbroken horizon, but only a faint streak, for, quite plausibly, she might merely have been bored with herself and come to pay a call on Tatiana Karl. Still, Tatiana was wondering why, why she was there. It was inevitable: she had nothing to say to Tatiana, nothing to tell, she seemed only to have the vaguest recollection, virtually no memory at all, of their school days together, and her ten years in Uxbridge required no more than ten minutes to sum up.

I was the only one to realize, because of that immense, half-starved look she had given me while she had been embracing Tatiana, that there was a specific purpose behind her visit here. How was that possible? I had my doubts. In order to derive an even greater pleasure in remembering exactly how she had looked at me, I persisted in doubting. It was completely different from her expression at present. There remained no trace of it. But her indifference toward me now was too obvious to be natural. She studiously avoided looking at me. Nor did I say anything to her.

"In what way were people wrong?" Tatiana said at last.

Tense, not liking to be interrogated in this way, she none the less made this reply, profoundly sorry to disappoint Tatiana:

"About the reasons," she said, "they were wrong about the reasons."

"That I knew," Tatiana said, "I mean . . . I suspected as much. Things are never as simple . . ."

Once again Peter Beugner changed the subject. Obviously he was the only one of us who could not bear to see Lol's face when she spoke of her youth. He began talking again, talking to her about what? about how beautiful her garden was, and her lawn, he explained that he had passed by her house and seen it, and what a marvelous idea it was to have planted that hedge between her house and that street with its heavy traffic!

She seemed to sense something, to suspect that there was more than a purely platonic relationship between Tatiana and me. Whenever Tatiana turns her attention from Lol for a moment, when she leaves off questioning her, it becomes more apparent: whenever she is in the presence of one of her lovers, Tatiana is inevitably affected by the always recent memory of her afternoons in the Forest Hotel. Whenever she gets to her feet, moves from one spot to another, whenever she rearranges her hair, or sits down, her movements are sensual. Her girlish body, her wound, her happy misery, cries out, calls for the paradise of her lost unity, calls endlessly, now and forever, for someone to console her and comfort her, her body is whole only in a hotel bed.

Tatiana serves tea. Lol's eyes follow her. We are both watching her, Lol and I. Any other aspect of Tatiana becomes secondary. In Lol's eyes, and in mine, she is nothing but Jack Hold's mistress. I have a difficult time following what they are both reminiscing about now, in a bantering tone, something about their youth, about Tatiana's hair. Lol says:

"Ah, when you unpinned your hair and let it down in the evening, the whole dormitory would come and watch. We used to give you a hand."

It will never be a question of Lol's blondness, nor of her blue eyes, never.

I intend to find out why, no matter what I have to do, why, why me?

Then this happened. As Tatiana is once again arranging her hair I am thinking back to yesterday—Lol is watching her—I remember my head buried in her breast, yesterday. I have no idea that Lol saw us, and yet the way she is watching Tatiana is what prompts me to remember. It seems to me I already know a trifle more about what is going on inside Tatiana when, naked, she rearranges her hair in the room in the Forest Hotel.

What was this unruffled ghost concealing about a love so deep, so strong, they said, that it had literally driven her mad? I was on my guard. She is soft and gentle, smiling, she is speaking of Tatiana Karl.

Personally, Tatiana did not believe that Lol Stein's insanity could be traced back solely to that ball, she traced its origins back further, further in Lol's life, back to her youth, she saw it as stemming from somewhere else. In school, she says, there was something lacking in Lol, she was already then strangely incomplete, she had lived her early years as though she were waiting for something she might, but never did, become. In school, she was a marvel of gentleness and indifference, she changed friends with abandon, she never made the least effort to combat boredom, nor had she ever been known to shed a sentimental schoolgirl's tear. When the rumor of her engagement to Michael Richardson first became known, she, Tatiana, had only half believed it. Who could Lol have found, who could ever have captured her so completely? or at least to a sufficient degree to entice her into marriage? who could have captured her unfinished heart? Does Tatiana still believe she was wrong?

I also seem to remember Tatiana's telling me some

bits of gossip, lots of gossip, rumors that had been rife in South Tahla at the time of Lol Stein's marriage. Didn't one rumor have it that she was already pregnant with her first daughter? I can't remember exactly, this one, and the others like it, are nothing but a confused murmur in the distance which I can no longer distinguish from the tales that Tatiana tells at present. Now, I alone of all these perverters of the truth know this: that I know nothing. That was my initial discovery about her: to know nothing about Lol Stein was already to know her. One could, it seemed to me, know even less about her, less and less about Lol Stein.

Some time went by. Lol stayed on, happy still, but not convincing any of us that it was because she had seen Tatiana again.

"Do you ever have occasion to come by the house?" Tatiana asks.

Lol says that she sometimes does, she goes out walking every day, in the afternoon, today however she made a point of coming, she had written several letters to the school and then to Tatiana's parents, after she had come across that photograph.

Why was she staying on and on?

It is now evening.

In the evening, Tatiana always grew sad. She could never forget. Again tonight she glanced outside: the white standard of lovers on their maiden voyage still floats over the darkened city. No longer is defeat Tatiana's lot, she bursts forth, pours over the universe. She says that she would have liked to take a trip. She asks Lol if she feels the same way. Lol says that she hasn't ever given the matter any thought.

"Perhaps I would, but where?"

"You'll find some place," Tatiana says.

They could not get over the fact that they had never run into each other in the center of town. But the fact is, Tatiana says, that she does not go out a great deal at this time of year, and when she does it's generally to pay a visit to her parents. That's not true. Tatiana has plenty of free time. I take up all of Tatiana's free time.

Lol is recounting the story of her life subsequent to her marriage: the birth of her children, her vacations. She gives a detailed, room-by-room description— maybe that's what she thinks we want to know—of the house she had formerly lived in in Uxbridge, a description that goes on so long that, once again, Tatiana and Peter Beugner begin to grow uncomfortable. I listen, hanging on her every word. Actually, she is telling about how a dwelling becomes empty when she moves in.

"The living room is so big that we could have given a dance in it. I was never able to do a thing with it, nothing I tried in the way of furnishings seemed to work."

She goes on with her descriptions. She is talking of Uxbridge. Suddenly she is no longer doing it to please or impress us, like some little girl reciting her lessons, the way she must have promised herself she would. Her words are flowing faster, her voice is louder, her eyes are no longer upon us: she is saying that the ocean is not far from that house they used to live in in Uxbridge. Tatiana gives a start: the ocean's a good two hours from Uxbridge. But Lol notices nothing.

"I mean, if it weren't for the new buildings that

have gone up we could have seen the beach from my bedroom window."

She goes on to describe that room, and the slip is forgotten. She comes back to Town Beach, which she does not confuse with anything else, again she is present among us, in full possession of all her faculties.

"Some day I'll go back there, there's no reason why I shouldn't."

I wanted to see her eyes on me again: I say:

"Why not go back there sometime this summer?"

She looked at me, the way I wanted her to. This look, which slipped away from her, altered her train of thought. She answered vaguely:

"Perhaps this year. I used to love the beach"—to Tatiana—"do you remember?"

Her eyes are like velvet, the way only dark eyes can be, hers now are a mixture of still water and silt, revealing nothing at present except a kind of drowsy sweetness.

"You still have that sweet, gentle expression you always had," Tatiana says.

Here, in a smile, here is a kind of joyous mockery which, to my mind, is inappropriate. Tatiana suddenly recognizes something.

"Ah!" she says, "that's the way you used to make fun of people whenever anyone told you that."

Perhaps she had just fallen asleep for a long moment.

"I wasn't making fun. You thought I was. How lovely you are, Tatiana! Ah, how well I remember!"

Tatiana got up to embrace Lol. Another woman took over in her stead, unforseeable, out of place, unrecognizable. Whom was she making fun of, if indeed she was?

I had to know her, because such was her desire. The pink of her cheeks is for me, she smiles for me, her ironic comments are meant for me. It is warm, suddenly we are stifling in Tatiana's living room. I say:

"You're beautiful too."

With a movement of her head, an abrupt movement, as though I had slapped her, she turns to me:

"Do you think so?"

"Yes," says Peter Beugner.

She laughs again.

"How ridiculous!"

Tatiana becomes solemn. She contemplates her friend attentively. I realize that she is virtually certain that Lol is not completely recovered. I can see that this is profoundly reassuring to her; even this pale vestige of Lol's insanity puts a halt to the terrible swift flight of things, slows to some slight extent the insensate flight of past summers.

"Your voice is different," Tatiana says, "but I would have recognized your laugh anywhere."

Lol says:

"Don't worry, there's no need to worry, Tatiana."

With eyes lowered, she waited. No one answered her. It was to me that she had spoken.

Curious, amused, she leaned over to Tatiana.

"What did my voice used to be like? I can't really remember."

"A trifle harsh. You used to speak fast. We had trouble understanding you."

Lol burst out laughing.

"I was hard of hearing," she says, "but no one knew it. My voice was the voice of someone who can't hear."

On Thursdays, Tatiana relates, they both used to balk at marching in schoolgirl file with the rest of the students, they used to dance instead in the empty playground—shall we dance, Tatiana?—a record player in a neighboring building, always the same one, used to play a medley of old-fashioned dance tunes, a nostalgic program they used to look forward to, the school monitors were gone, there they were alone in the vast school yard where, that day, they could hear the street noises. Come on, Tatiana, come on, let's dance; sometimes, in a fit of exasperation, they play, they shout, they try to frighten each other.

We watched her as she listened to Tatiana and seemed to call upon me to verify the truth of this past. Is that really it? Is that the way it really was?

"Tatiana has told us about those Thursdays," says Peter Beugner.

Tatiana, as she does every day, has let the semi-darkness settle down, and I have a chance to study Lol Stein at length, at sufficient length, before she leaves, so that I shall never forget her.

When Tatiana switched on the lights, Lol reluctantly got to her feet. To what fictitious home was she returning? I still didn't know.

Once she is up, on the verge of leaving, she finally says what she had to say: she wants to see Tatiana again.

"I want to see you again, Tatiana."

Then, what should have appeared natural seems false. I lower my eyes. Tatiana, who is trying to catch my attention, loses it like a lost coin. Why does Lol, who seems fully able to get along without needing anyone, want to see me, Tatiana, again? I go out onto the steps. It is not yet completely dark, I realize, far from it. I hear Tatiana asking:

"Why do you want to see me again? Did that photograph make you want to see me again all that much? I'm intrigued."

I turn around: Lol doesn't know which way to turn, her eyes search for mine, she hesitates between a lie and the truth and, courageously, opts for the lie.

"That photograph was part of it," she adds, "and besides, I'm supposed to get out and meet people nowadays."

Tatiana laughs:

"That's hardly like you, Lola."

I learn that nothing can match Lol's unaffected laugh when she is lying. She says:

"We'll see, we'll see where it will all lead to. I feel so much at home with you."

"Yes, we'll see," Tatiana says gaily.

"You know you don't have to see me again, I'll understand."

"I know," Tatiana says.

A touring theatrical company was in South Tahla that week. Wouldn't that be a good opportunity to get together again? They could go to the theatre and then come back to Lol's afterward, to meet John Bedford.

Couldn't Peter Beugner and Jack Hold join them as well?

Tatiana had a moment of hesitation, then she said that she would come, she would give up her plans to go to the shore. Peter Beugner was free. I'll do my best, I say, to cancel a previous dinner engagement. That same evening Tatiana and I have a rendezvous at the Forest Hotel.

The following day I phoned Tatiana and told her that we would not be going to the Bedfords. She thought I was sincere. She told me that it was impossible for her not to accept Lol's invitation this first time.

John Bedford has retired to his room. He has a concert tomorrow. He has some exercises to run through on the violin.

At this point of the evening it is about half-past eleven, and we are in the children's playroom. It is a large bare room, with a billiard table. The children's toys are in one corner, stacked away in boxes. The bil-

liard table is very old, it must have already been in the
Stein family before Lol was born.

Peter Beugner is playing billiards. I am watching
him. When we left the theatre, he told me that we
should leave Tatiana and Lol alone together for awhile
before rejoining them. It seemed likely, he had added,
that Lol had some deep dark secret to reveal to Tatiana, which would explain why she had been so insist-
ent about seeing her again.

I circle the billiard table. The windows looking out
over the garden are open. A large door which leads out
onto a lawn is also open. The room is next to John
Bedford's room. Lol and Tatiana can hear the violin—
as we can—but for them it is less loud. A vestibule
separates them from these two rooms where the men
are. They can no doubt also hear the dull click of the
billiard balls as they strike each other. John Bedford's
exercises on two strings are high-pitched and piercing.
Their monotonous frenzy is wildly musical, the song of
the instrument itself.

The weather is beautiful. But Lol, contrary to cus-
tom, has shut the bay windows in the living room.
When we reached the darkened house, with its open
windows, she told Tatiana, who was surprised to see
them that way, that she was in the habit of leaving
them open at this time of year. But not tonight. Why?
Tatiana probably asked her why. Tatiana's the one
who wants to open her heart to Lol, this heart we two
never allude to between us, and not vice-versa, that
much I know.

Lol has shown Tatiana her three sleeping children.
We heard their muffled laughter echoing on the floor

above. And then they came back downstairs to the living room. We were already in the billiard room. I don't know whether Lol was surprised to find us gone. We heard the three bay windows being closed.

She, on the other side of the vestibule, and I, here in this game room, whose floor I am pacing, are waiting to see each other again.

It was an amusing play. The women laughed a lot. On three occasions, Lol and I were the only ones laughing. During intermission, as I was passing Tatiana and John Bedford, I was able to gather that they were talking, in a brief aside, about Lol.

I leave the billiard room. Peter doesn't even notice me go. We make it a rule not to remain alone together for too long at a time, because of Tatiana. I have a strong suspicion that Peter Beugner isn't as oblivious as Tatiana would like to think. I skirt the house, and in a few steps find myself outside one of the lateral bay windows of the living room.

Lol is seated facing that bay window. She does not yet see me. The living room is smaller than the billiard room, and is furnished with a number of unmatching easy chairs and a large glass case of black wood which houses books and a butterfly collection. The walls are bare, painted white. Everything is meticulously clean, rectilinear in its arrangement, most of the chairs are flush against the walls, and the light, which is inadequate, comes from ceiling fixtures.

Lol gets up and offers Tatiana a glass of sherry. She, Lol, is not yet drinking. Tatiana seems to be on the verge of confiding something to Lol. She is speaking, then breaks off what she is saying, lowers her eyes, says

something, no, that's not yet it. Lol moves about, tries
to parry the blow. She does not want Tatiana's secrets,
she wouldn't know what to do with them, one even has
the impression they would embarrass her. She has us in
her hands. Why? How? I have no idea.

I have no plans for meeting Tatiana again at the
Forest Hotel until the day after tomorrow, yes, two
days from now. I would like to make it tonight, after
we leave Lol's. I have a feeling that tonight my desire
for Tatiana will be sated forever, the task accom-
plished, however arduous, long, and difficult it may be,
however exhausting, at which point I shall be faced
with a certainty.

Which certainty? It will probably involve Lol, but
how I don't know, nor do I know what it will mean,
what physical or mental part of Lol will be illuminated
as a result of my gratified desire for Tatiana, nor have I
even tried to stop and figure it out.

Now Tatiana gets up, says something very heatedly.
At first Lol steps back, then she comes back over close
to Tatiana and lightly strokes her hair.

Up until the very last minute, I tried to entice
Tatiana to the Forest Hotel, whereas it was Lol I was
supposed to see again. I couldn't do that to a friend,
Tatiana said, after such a long absence, what she's been
through in the past, and that fragility, too, did you
notice how fragile she was? No, I can't turn down that
invitation. Tatiana thought I was being sincere. In a
little while, shortly, in two short days I shall possess all
of Tatiana Karl, possess her completely, until there's
nothing left to possess.

Lol is still stroking Tatiana's hair. At first she gazes

at her intently, but then she is staring vacantly into
space, she is stroking the way some blind person in
search of her bearings might. Then it's Tatiana's turn
to step back. Lol raises her eyes, and I can see her lips
forming the name: Tatiana Karl. Her expression is
tender, opaque. Her look, which was meant for Tatiana, falls upon me: she notices me outside the bay
window. She shows no sign of emotion. Tatiana fails to
notice anything. Lol moves forward, toward Tatiana,
she comes back, puts her arm around her lightly and,
without seeming to, leads her toward the French doors
which open onto the grounds. She opens it. I see what
she wants. I move forward, keeping to the wall. There.
I'm at the corner of the house. From this point I can
hear what they are saying. Suddenly, here are their
voices, interwoven, tender, diluted by the night, simi-
larly feminine voices which seem but one voice when
they reach me. I can hear both of them. That is what
Lol wanted. It is she who is speaking:

"Look at all these trees, these beautiful trees of ours.
How lovely it is out."

"Tell me, Lola, what was hardest for you?" Tatiana
asks.

"Keeping to a regular schedule. For the children, for
meals, for sleep."

Tatiana gives a long, plaintive, weary sigh.

"To this day my house is an ungodly mess. I have a
rich husband, no children, so, really . . . what's the
point? . . ."

Lol, with the same gentle movement she had used
before, guides Tatiana back to the center of the living
room. I return to my post at the bay window from

where I can observe them. I can hear them and I can see them. She offers her a chair in such a way that her back will be to the garden. She sits down opposite her. The entire span of the bay windows is directly in her line of vision. If she chooses to look she can. She does not look, not once.

"Do you have any urge to change, Tatiana?"

Tatiana shrugs her shoulders and does not reply, at least nothing I can hear.

"You're wrong, Tatiana. Don't change, don't, you really shouldn't."

Tatiana now:

"There were two choices open to me from the start: to live the way we used to when we were young, open to a whole range of possibilities, you remember, or else settle down into a fixed pattern, the way you have, you know what I mean, please don't take offense, but you know."

Lol listens. She has not forgotten my presence, but she is truly divided between the two of us. She says:

"I never had a chance to choose my life. It was a good thing I didn't, people used to say, what would I have done if I'd had to make a choice? But now I can't conceive of any other life I might have had in the place of this one. Tatiana, I'm terribly happy tonight."

This time it's Tatiana who gets up and puts her arm around Lol. I can see them clearly. Lol offers some slight resistance to Tatiana's affectionate gesture, but Tatiana probably attributes it to Lol's modesty. She does not take offense. Lol breaks away and goes to the middle of the room. I step back, against the wall. The next time I look in, they are back in their respective chairs.

"Listen to John. Sometimes he'll practice till four in the morning. He's completely forgotten us."

"Do you always listen?"

"Almost always. Especially when I . . ."

Tatiana is waiting. The rest of the sentence doesn't follow. Tatiana continues:

"And what about the future, Lol? Don't you ever imagine anything . . . anything a bit different?"

How full of affection Tatiana's words are!

Lol has poured herself a glass of sherry and is drinking in little sips. She is reflecting.

"I don't know yet," she says at length. "I take the days one at a time, as they come. The house is so big. There's always something new I have to look after. It's difficult not to. Oh, I'm referring simply to household matters, you know, errands to run and shopping to do."

Tatiana laughs.

"You can't be serious," she says.

Again she gets up and circles the living room, a trifle impatient. Lol remains where she was. I move back, out of sight. I can no longer see what they are doing. She must by now have come back to her place. Yes.

"What kind of errands?" she asks harshly.

Lol raises her head, is terrified. I contemplate bursting into the room and obliging Tatiana to shut up. Lol responds immediately, her tone a trifle guilty:

"Oh, some pieces of china impossible to match, for one thing. You keep on hoping some store in the suburbs will have the pattern you want."

"John Bedford mentioned something about an errand you went on last week out in the suburbs . . . somewhere way out . . . and you got home so late . . . goodness! Tell me, is that true, Lol?"

"In that short space of time he managed to tell you all that?"

I move from one bay window to another, to see or hear better. Lol's voice no longer betrays any trace of concern. She has simply turned a shade more toward Tatiana. What she is about to say does not interest her. She seems to be listening, listening for something that Tatiana cannot hear: my movements to and fro along the walls.

"It happened quite naturally. We were talking about you, your life, about your finicky habits, which seem to worry him slightly. Were you aware of that?"

"He's never mentioned it to me, at least not that I remember," Lol says. "I have a feeling he likes to see me go out"—she then adds: "Listen to the music, and to them playing billiards. They've forgotten about us too. We don't do much entertaining, especially this late. I really do enjoy it, though."

"You wanted to buy some shrubs, didn't you? some plants for a hedge?" Tatiana asks, this time a little too casually.

"One of John's friends told me that in this region some people had succeeded in growing pomegranates. So I began to keep an eye out for some."

"You had one chance in a thousand of finding any, Lol."

"No," Lol says gravely, "not even one."

This lie doesn't bother Tatiana. On the contrary.

Lol is lying. Careful this time, taking due precaution to vary her approach, Tatiana ventures to touch on another area, further back in time.

"Were we actually such close friends in school? How do we look in that photograph?"

Lol seems distressed.

"I'm afraid I've mislaid it again," she says.

Now Tatiana knows for sure: Lol Stein is also lying to her. The lie is glaring, incomprehensible, totally inexplicable. Lol is smiling at Tatiana. It is as though Tatiana is giving up, as though she has made up her mind not even to try and understand.

"I can't really remember now whether we were such close friends," Lol says.

"In school," Tatiana says. "Don't you remember being in school?"

Tatiana is staring fixedly at Lol: is she going to dismiss her from her life forever or, on the contrary, see her again, be anxious to see her again? Lol is still smiling at her, with a vague, indifferent smile. Is she with me now, behind the bay windows? or somewhere else?

"I don't remember," she says. "Not about any friendship. I don't remember anything of the kind."

I have the impression that she realizes that she ought to watch her step, that she is somewhat frightened by what is going to come next. I can see it in her eyes, which are searching for mine. Tatiana still hasn't seen anything. She says—now it's her turn to lie—she ventures:

"I'm not sure whether I'll be able to see you as often as you would apparently like."

Lol's response is a veritable supplication:

"Ah," she says, "you'll see, just wait, Tatiana, you'll get used to me."

"The problem is, I have lovers," Tatiana says. "My lovers occupy every minute of my free time. Which is the way I want it."

Lol sits down. Her expression is one of sadness, mixed with discouragement.

"I didn't realize," she says softly, "I didn't realize you used such words, Tatiana."

She gets up. She tiptoes away from Tatiana as though she were concerned not to wake some sleeping child close by. Tatiana follows her, feeling a bit contrite because of what she takes to be Lol's increasing depression. They are both by the window, very close to where I am standing.

"What is your opinion of our friend Jack Hold?"

Lol turns till she is facing the grounds. Her voice is louder, without expression, incantatory:

"The best man in the world is dead for me. I have no opinion."

They fall silent. Their backs are to me, I see them both framed by the curtains of the French doors. Tatiana murmurs:

"After all these years. I wanted to ask you, Lol, whether . . ."

I fail to catch the rest of Tatiana's sentence because I am now moving toward the doorstep where Lol is standing, her back to the garden. Lol's voice is still clear, resonant. She means to escape the aura of intimate revelation, wants to make her words public.

"I don't know," she says, "I don't know whether I still think about it."

She turns around, smiles, says almost without any break from what she has just said:

"Why, here's Mr. Hold. I thought you were in the billiard room."

"I was until a moment ago."

I advance into the light. To Tatiana, it all seems quite natural.

"You look as though you're cold," she says to me.

Lol ushers us into the room. She pours me a glass of sherry, which I drink. Tatiana is lost in her thoughts. Is she upset, however slightly, because I happened on the scene too soon? No, she is too deeply absorbed by Lol to be upset. Lol, her hands on her knees, leaning forward in a familiar posture, directs her words to Tatiana:

"Love," she says, "I remember."

Tatiana is staring into space.

"That ball, Lol! oh, that ball!"

Lol, without shifting position, stares into the same void as Tatiana.

"What?" she asks. "How do you know?"

Tatiana has a moment of doubt. Then at last she cries out:

"But Lol, I was there the whole night, there beside you!"

Lol evinces no surprise, nor does she even try to remember, it's no use.

"Ah! So it was you," she says. "I'd forgotten."

Does Tatiana believe her? She hesitates, darts a sidelong glance at Lol, quivering, her hopes more than confirmed. Then Lol, with a kind of pitiful curiosity, a century-old refugee from her youth, asks:

"Did I suffer? Tell me, Tatiana, I've never really known."

Tatiana says:

"No."

She slowly shakes her head, for a long time.

"No. I'm your only witness. I can tell you that you didn't. You were smiling at them. You weren't suffering."

Lol's fingers dig into her cheeks. Lost in that ball, entrapped, they both are completely oblivious of my presence.

"I remember," she says, "I must have been smiling."

I move past them in the room. Neither one says anything.

I leave. I head for the billiard room, in search of Peter.

"They're waiting for us."

"I was looking for you."

"I was out on the lawn. Come, let's join them."

"You think it's all right?"

"I have a feeling it doesn't matter to them whether they talk in our presence. They may even prefer it."

We enter the living room. They are both still silent.

"Aren't you going to call John Bedford?"

Lol gets up, goes out into the vestibule, closes a door —the sound of the violin is suddenly softer.

"He'd just as soon not be with us tonight."

She pours us all some sherry, and serves herself. Peter Beugner downs his in a single draft, the silence terrifies him, he can't bear it.

"I think it's time we were leaving," he says, "whenever Tatiana is ready."

"Oh, no! not yet," Lol begs.

I am standing, I wander restlessly about the room, my eyes upon her. The thing ought to be obvious. But Tatiana is plunged deep into the Town Beach ball. She has no desire to leave, nor has she even bothered to reply to her husband. This ball was also Tatiana's. Oblivious to all around her, she is once again seeing a person who was there.

"John is becoming more and more of a fanatic about his music," Lol says. "Sometimes he goes on playing till the wee hours of the morning. In fact, it happens more and more often."

"He's a man people are talking about, I've heard people mention his concerts," Peter Beugner says. "It's rare that his name doesn't crop up in the course of a dinner or a party."

"Yes, that's true," I say.

Lol is talking in order to keep them, to keep me, searching for some way to make my task easier. Tatiana is not listening.

"In fact, Tatiana, you were talking about him," says Peter Beugner, "because he married Lol."

Lol sits down on the edge of her chair, prepared to get to her feet if anyone makes a move to leave.

"John got married under somewhat unusual circumstances, that some people found rather amusing. That's probably another reason why people talk about him, they remember our marriage."

Then I address my question to Tatiana:

"What was Michael Richardson like?"

They are not surprised, they look at each other, endlessly, endlessly, decide that it is impossible to describe, to give an account of those moments, of that evening whose veritable depth and density they, and they alone, are familiar with, that night whose hours they had seen slip by, one by one, until the last had gone, and, by that last hour, love had changed hands, identity, one error had been exchanged for another.

"He never came back, never," Tatiana says. "What a mad night!"

"Came back?"

"He has no ties left in Town Beach. His parents are dead, and he's sold whatever they left him. He's never once set foot in Town Beach again."

"I knew that," Lol says.

Their words are for themselves alone. The sound of the violin can still be heard. It is fairly obvious that John Bedford is also practicing to avoid having to be with us this evening.

"Do you think he may be dead?"

"He may be. He was as dear to you as life itself."

Lol's reply is a slight pout, indicating doubt.

"What about the police, why did the police come?"

Tatiana glances at us, somewhat startled, frightened: this is one fact she didn't know.

"No, your mother mentioned the police, but they never came."

She is reflecting. And it is when she does that the obscurity returns. But it returns only for the ball, never for anything else.

"That's strange, I thought they had. Did he really have to leave?"

"When?"

"In the morning?"

Lol Stein grew up here in South Tahla, her father was originally from Germany, he was a professor of history at the university, her mother was from South Tahla, Lol has a brother nine years her elder, he lives in Paris, she never makes the slightest allusion to this one relative, Lol met the man from Town Beach one morning during summer vacation, at the tennis courts, he was twenty-five, the only son of well-to-do parents whose land holdings in the area were extensive, he had no vocation, was a cultured, brilliant, extremely brilliant person, a moody, saturnine man, Lol fell in love with him the moment she saw him.

"Seeing that he had changed, he had to leave."

"The woman," Tatiana says, "was Anne-Marie Stretter, she was French, the wife of the French Consul in Calcutta."

"Is she dead?"

"No. She's old."

"How do you know?"

"I sometimes see her during the summer. She spends a few days in Town Beach. It's all over. She never left her husband. Their affair must have lasted only a short while, no more than a few months."

"A few months," Lol repeats.

Tatiana takes Lol's hands, lowers her voice:

"Listen to me, Lol, listen to me now. Why do you say things that aren't true? Are you doing it on purpose?"

"People around me," Lol begins again, "people around me were mistaken about the reasons."

"Answer me."

"I lied."

I ask:

"When?"

"All the time."

"When you shouted?"

Lol makes no move to retreat, she places herself in Tatiana's care. None of us moves a muscle, the two women have forgotten us.

"No. Not then."

"Did you want them to stay?"

"What?" Lol says.

"What did you want?"

Lol does not reply. No one presses her to. Then she answers me:

"I wanted to see them."

I go out onto the steps. I wait for her. From the first minute, when the two women embraced on the path in front of the terrace, I have been waiting for Lol Stein. She wants me to wait. Tonight, by keeping us here, she is playing with fire, she is delaying, postponing this wait, one has the impression that she is still waiting in Town Beach for what is going to happen here. I'm mistaken. Where are we heading with her? One can be consistently wrong, but no, I'm ceasing to be: she wants to see, and to have me witness with her, the darkness of tomorrow, which will be the darkness of the night of Town Beach, advance upon us, swallow us up. She is the night of Town Beach. Later, in a little while, when I kiss her on the mouth, the door will open and I shall go through it. Peter Beugner is listening, he is no longer talking about leaving, his embarrassment has disappeared.

"He was younger than she was," Tatiana is saying,

"but by the time the night was over they both seemed to be the same age. We all were old, infinitely old. You were the oldest."

Each time one of them speaks, a floodgate opens. I know that the last one will never be reached.

"Did you notice, Tatiana, at the end, while they were dancing, they said something to each other?"

"I did notice, but I didn't hear what they said."

"I did: 'maybe it will kill her.' "

"No. You couldn't have heard them. You were there with me the whole time, behind the green plants at the end of the room."

Lol is coming back. Here she is, suddenly indifferent, distracted.

"You mean the woman who was caressing my hand was you, Tatiana?"

"Yes, it was."

"No one"—she sighs—"no one had thought of that!"

I come back inside. They both know that I haven't missed a single word.

"When it began to grow light out he looked around for you, but he couldn't find you. Did you know that?"

Lol knew nothing.

There is no way of approaching Lol. One can neither get close to her or move away from her. You have to wait until she comes in search of you, until she wants to. What she wants, I now understand clearly, is to be seen and encountered by me in a certain space, a setting she is presently arranging. What setting? Is it peopled by ghosts from Town Beach, by the only survivor, Tatiana, filled with pretenses, with twenty

women all bearing the name of Lol? Or is it different?
In a little while I shall be formally introduced to Lol,
by Lol. How is she going to manage to bring me close
to her?

"For ten years I've been under the impression that
there were only three people left: the two of them, and
me."

I ask again:

"What is it you wanted?"

With precisely the same hesitation as before, the
same interval of silence, she replies:

"To see them."

I see everything. I see love itself. Lol's eyes are
stabbed by the light: all around, a dark circle. I see
both the light and the dark which surrounds it. She
keeps advancing toward me, at the same pace. She cannot advance any faster, or any slower. The slightest
modification in her movement would seem to me to be
a catastrophe, the definitive defeat of our affair: no one
would be there for the assignation.

But what is there about me I am so completely unaware of and which she summons me to know? who
will be there, at that moment, beside her?

She is coming. Keeps on coming, even with the
others present. No one sees her coming.

She is still talking about Michael Richardson, they
had finally understood, they were searching for some
way to leave the ball, they went in the wrong direction,
heading for imaginary doors.

Whenever she speaks, whenever she moves, when
she looks or is lost in thought, I have the feeling that I
am witnessing with my own eyes some personal and

capital manner of lying, an immense yet strictly limited field of lies. For us, this woman is lying about
Town Beach, about South Tahla, about this evening,
for me, for us, in a little while she will lie about our
meeting, that I can foresee, she is lying about herself
too, because the abyss between us, between her and the
three of us, she alone is responsible for—but in silence
—in a dream so compelling that it has escaped her, and
she is unaware she ever had it.

I desperately want to partake of the word which
emerges from the lips of Lol Stein, I want to be a part
of this lie which she has forged. Let her bear me with
her, let our affair take, from this point forth, a different
course, let her consume and crush me with the rest, I
shall bend to her will, let my hope be to be crushed
with the rest, to be bent to her will.

A prolonged silence ensues. The reason for the silence is our growing interest one for the other. No one
is aware of it, no one yet; no one? am I quite sure?

Lol starts out toward the steps, slowly, then walks
back, just as slowly.

Seeing her, it occurs to me that that will perhaps
suffice for me, simply to see her and leave it at that,
that it will be pointless to carry the matter any further,
either in gesture or in word. My hands are becoming
the trap wherewith to ensnare her, immobilize her,
keep her from constantly moving to and fro from one
end of time to the other.

"It's terribly late, and Peter has to get up early,"
Tatiana finally says.

She thought that Lol's movement toward the door
was an invitation to leave.

"No, please don't go," Lol says. "When I closed John's door he didn't even notice, no, please don't go, Tatiana."

"You'll have to offer him our apologies," Tatiana says. "It's not important, really."

It is done, the course of events has escaped me, I was looking at Lol: Tatiana's expression is hard now. Things are not going the way she would have liked. She has just discovered it: Lol is keeping something to herself. And is there not, in the room, between one and the other of us, something akin to a clandestine traffic, an odor of that poison she fears above all else when she is present, an understanding from which she is excluded?

"Something's happening in this house, Lol," she says with a forced smile. "Or is that only my impression? Is it possible you could be expecting someone you're afraid of, so late at night? Why are you keeping us here like this?"

"Someone who would be coming to see you alone," says Peter Beugner. He laughs.

"Oh! that's hardly likely," Lol says.

She has that mocking air that Tatiana no longer finds funny. No. Again I'm mistaken. Tatiana is completely in the dark.

"Actually, if you must leave, please do. It's just that I would have enjoyed having your company a bit longer tonight."

"You're keeping something from us, Lol," Tatiana says.

"Even if Lol were to reveal this secret to us," Peter Beugner says, "it might not be the secret she thinks it is, in spite of what she thinks, it might be different from . . ."

I hear myself saying:

"Stop it!"

Tatiana remains unruffled. Again I'm mistaken. Tatiana says:

"It's so late, things are getting all mixed up. You'll have to forgive him. Tell us something, Lol."

Lol Stein is resting, it would appear, resting for a moment from the exertion of a victory which might have been too easily won. One thing of which I am certain is the price of that victory: the retreat of clarity. For anyone except us, her eyes would seem to be too bright, too gay.

She says, without addressing anyone in particular:

"It's because I'm happy."

She flushes. She laughs. The word amuses her.

"Anyway, now you can leave," she adds.

"Can't you tell us why?" Tatiana asks.

"It wouldn't make any sense, it would be pointless."

Tatiana is tapping her foot.

"Still," she says, "tell us something, just a word or two about this happiness."

"A few days ago I met someone," Lol says. "My happiness stems from that encounter."

Tatiana gets to her feet. Peter Beugner gets up in turn. They both go over to Lol.

"Ah! so that's it," Tatiana says, "so that's it."

She has just had a brush with terror, which terror I cannot say, but her smile is the smile of a convalescent. She almost shouts:

"Be careful, Lol, oh, Lol, watch your step!"

Lol also gets up. Directly facing her, behind Tatiana, is Jack Hold, me. He was mistaken, he is thinking. He's not the one Lol Stein is looking for. She is looking for someone else. Lol says:

"Nothing about that affair of mine when I was young bothers me. Even if I had to go through it again, it wouldn't bother me."

"Be careful, be careful, Lol."

Tatiana turns around to Jack Hold.

"Are you coming?"

Jack Hold says:

"No."

Tatiana looks at both of them, first one then the other.

"My, my," she says, "you mean to say you intend to keep Lol Stein's happiness company?"

She comes back from seeing the Beugners to the door. She comes in, slowly, and leans against the French doors. With bowed head, her hands behind her gripping the curtains, she remains there. I feel I am going to fall. I can sense my body growing weak, some sort of level is rising, drowning the blood, my heart is of silt, goes soft, turns to sludge, is going to sleep. Who could she have met in my place?

"So, what about that encounter?"

The poor woman in her black dress is thin and bowed. She lifts her hand, calls to me.

"Ah! Jack Hold, I was sure you had guessed."

She steels herself for a violent outburst. For all hell to break loose.

"Tell me anyway, do."

"Tell you what?"

"Who it is."

"It's you, you, Jack Hold. I met you seven days ago, at first when you were alone, then later when you were with a woman. I followed you to the Forest Hotel."

I had a moment of fear. I wanted to return to Tatiana, to be in the street.

"Why?"

She lets go of the curtains, straightens up, comes toward me.

"I picked you."

She is coming, looking, this is the first time we have been close to each other. She is white, stark white. She kisses me on the mouth. I give her nothing in return. I was too frightened, I can't yet. She anticipated that impossibility. I am in the night of Town Beach. It is all over. There, nothing is given to Lol Stein. She takes. I still feel like running away.

"But what is it you want?"

She doesn't know.

"I want . . ." she says.

She falls silent, looks at my mouth. And then here we are, staring into each other's eyes. Despotically, irresistibly, she wants.

"Why?"

She shakes her head, murmurs my name.

"Jack Hold."

Lol's virginity uttering that name! Who, except her, Lol Stein, the so-called Lol Stein, had noticed the inconsistency of the belief in that person so named. A dazzling discovery of the name the others have abandoned, have failed to recognize, which was invisible, an inanity shared by all the men of South Tahla, as much a part of myself as the course of my blood through my veins. She has plucked me, taken me from the nest. For the first time my name, pronounced, names nothing.

"Lola Stein."

"Yes."

From somewhere beyond the burned-out ruins of her being, she greets me with a smile. Her choice implies no preference. I am the man from South Tahla she has decided to follow. Here we are, bound together inextricably. Our emptiness grows. We repeat our names to each other.

I move closer to this body. I want to touch it. First with my hands, then with my lips.

I've become awkward. Just as my hands touch Lol, the memory of an unknown man, now dead, comes back to me: he will serve as the eternal Richardson, the man from Town Beach, we will be mingled with him, willy-nilly, all together, we shall no longer be able to recognize one from the other, neither before, nor after, nor during, we shall lose sight of one another, forget our names, in this way we shall die for having forgotten—piece by piece, moment by moment, name by name—death. Paths open up. Her mouth opens upon mine. Her open hand, resting upon my arm, heralds a future both varied and unique, a radiant, harmonious hand whose fingers are bent, broken, as light as a feather and, for me, as new as a flower.

Her body is tall and beautiful, very straight, made taut by her constant effort to efface herself, a constant conformity to a certain mode of conduct learned when she was a child, the body of a grown-up schoolgirl. But her gentle humility is inscribed in her face, in every gesture of her hand when her fingers touch some object, or when they touch my hand.

"There are times when your eyes are such a bright blue. How fair you are."

Lol's hair has the same flower-like texture as her hands. Dazzled, she agrees with me.

"You're right."

Beneath her partly lowered eyelids, her eyes are shining. I shall have to get used to the rarified air in the vicinity of these tiny blue planets which attract, ensnare my gaze, until it is helpless.

"You were just coming out of a cinema. It was last Thursday. Do you remember how hot it was? You were holding your suitcoat in your hand."

I listen. The violin sounds keep slipping in between the words, repeating certain passages, then going on.

"You weren't even aware of it, you didn't know what to do with yourself. You had just emerged from that dark aisle in the cinema, where you had gone by yourself to kill a little time. You had plenty of time that day. Once out on the boulevard, you stared at all the women passing by."

"You're absolutely wrong!"

"Maybe I am," Lol cried.

Her voice is once again low-pitched and calm, the way it doubtless used to be when she was young, but it is still faint and solemnly slow. Without any urging from me she moves into my arms, her eyes closed, waiting for something else that is about to happen, that has to happen, her body already revealing that the solemn celebration is close at hand. Here it is, spoken almost in a whisper:

"The woman who arrived on the square where all the buses meet was Tatiana Karl."

I don't answer her.

"It was Tatiana. You're a man who sooner or later was bound to be drawn to her. I knew that."

Her eyelids are covered with fine droplets of perspiration. I kiss her closed eyes, they move beneath my lips, her eyes are hidden. I let her go. I leave her. I move to the opposite end of the room. She remains where she is. I want to find out something.

"You're sure it isn't because I look like Michael Richardson?"

"No, that's not the reason," Lol says. "Anyway you don't. No," she drags out her words, "I don't know what it is."

The sound of the violin ceases. We stop talking. It starts in again.

"The light went on in your room, and I saw Tatiana walk in front of the light. She was naked beneath her black hair."

She does not move, her eyes staring out into the garden, waiting. She has just said that Tatiana is naked beneath her dark hair. That sentence is the last to have been uttered. I hear: "naked beneath her dark hair,

naked, naked, dark hair." The last two words especially strike with a strange and equal intensity. It's true
that Tatiana was as Lol has just described her, naked
beneath her dark hair. She was that way in the locked
room, for her lover. The intensity of the sentence suddenly increases, the air around it has been rent, the
sentence explodes, it blows the meaning apart. I hear it
with a deafening roar, and I fail to understand it, I no
longer even understand that it means nothing.

Lol is still far from me, rooted to the floor, still
turned toward the garden, unblinking.

The nudity of Tatiana, already naked, intensifies
into an overexposed image which makes it increasingly
impossible to make any sense whatsoever out of it.

The void is statue. The pedestal is there: the sentence. The void is Tatiana naked beneath her dark
hair, the fact. It is transformed, poured out lavishly,
the fact no longer contains the fact, Tatiana emerges
from herself, spills through the open windows out over
the town, the roads, mire, liquid, tide of nudity. Here
she is, Tatiana Karl, suddenly naked beneath her hair,
between Lol Stein and me. The sentence has just faded
away, I can no longer hear any sound, only silence, the
sentence is dead at Lol's feet, Tatiana is back in her
place. I reach out and touch, like a blind man I touch
and fail to recognize anything I have already touched.
Lol is waiting for me to recognize something, not that I
be attuned to her vision but that I no longer be afraid
of Tatiana. I am no longer afraid. There are two of us,
now, beholding Tatiana naked beneath her dark hair.
Blindly, I say:

"An extraordinary lay, Tatiana."

There was a movement of her head. Lol's tone is one

I have never heard from her before, shrill and plaintive. The wild animal removed from its forest home sleeps, dreams of the equator of its birth, trembles in its sleep, its dream of sunlight, weeps.

"The best, the best one of them all, right?"

I say:

"The best."

I go to Lol Stein. I kiss her, lick her, breathe in the odor that is Lol, kiss her teeth. She does not move. She has grown beautiful. She says:

"What an amazing coincidence."

I do not reply. Again I leave her, standing there far from me, in the middle of the living room. She does not even seem to realize that I have moved away from her. Again I say:

"I'm going to leave Tatiana Karl."

She sinks to the floor without a word, and assumes a posture of infinite supplication.

"Please, I beg of you, implore you, don't leave her!"

I rush back over to her, lift her to her feet. Anyone else might have been fooled completely. There was not the slightest trace of pain on her face, which was beaming with confidence.

"What?"

"Please, I beg of you."

"Tell me why."

She says:

"I don't want you to."

We are locked in together somewhere. Every echo dies. I am beginning to understand, by slow degrees, inchingly slow. I see walls, smooth, offering nothing to grasp, they were not there a short while before, they have just risen around us. If someone offered to save

me, I would not even know what he was talking about.
My ignorance itself is locked in. Lol is standing before
me, again she is begging, suddenly I am weary of trans-
lating what she is saying.

"I won't leave Tatiana Karl."

"Good. You're supposed to see her again."

"Next Tuesday."

The violin stops. It withdraws, leaving behind it
open craters of immediate memory. I am frightened,
appalled by all other people but Lol.

"And you? When will I see you?"

She tells me Wednesday, sets a time and place.

I don't return home. Nothing is open in town. So I
walk to the Beugners' house and go in by the garden
gate. There is a light in Tatiana's window. I knock on
the window. She is used to my knock. She dresses
quickly. By now it's three in the morning. She is at
great pains not to make any noise, although I am certain Peter Beugner knows exactly what is going on.
But she's the one who insists on acting as though our
affair were some great secret. She thinks that in South
Tahla she passes for a dutiful and faithful wife. She
intends to keep her reputation intact.

"But what about Tuesday?" she asks.

"Tuesday too."

I parked the car a fair distance from the gate. We
drive past the Beugners' house with our lights out,
then head for the Forest Hotel. In the car, Tatiana
asks:

"How was Lol after we went home?"

"Rational."

When I went to the window of the room in the Forest Hotel, where I was waiting for Tatiana Karl, on Tuesday at the appointed hour, dusk was just descending, and when I thought I could discern, between the hotel and the foot of the hill, a gray form, a woman about whose grayish blondness there could be no doubt whatsoever, I had a violent reaction, although I had been prepared for any eventuality, a very violent reaction I could not immediately define, something between terror and disbelief, horror and pleasure, and I was tempted by turn to cry out some warning, offer help, thrust her away forever, or involve myself forever with Lol Stein in all her complexities, fall in love with her. I stifled a cry, prayed to God for help, I ran out of the room, retraced my steps, paced the floor like a caged animal, too much alone to love or not to love, sick, sick of my frightful inability to admit what was happening.

Then my emotion abated to some slight degree, it contracted, and I was able to contain it. This moment coincided with the one when I discovered that she too must have been able to see me.

I'm lying. I did not move from the window, my worst fears confirmed, fighting back the tears.

Suddenly the blondness was different than before, it moved then came to rest. I had the feeling she must have become aware that I had discovered her presence.

So we both looked at each other, or so I believed. For how long?

At my wit's end, I turned my head away, toward the right side of the rye field where she was not. From that direction, Tatiana, in a black suit, was arriving. She paid the taxi and started walking slowly past the alder trees.

Without knocking, she gently opened the door to the room. I asked her to come over and join me for a minute at the window. Tatiana came. I showed her the field of rye and the hill beyond. I was standing behind her. Thus it was that I showed her to Tatiana.

"We never look at the view. From this side of the hotel it's really quite beautiful."

Tatiana saw nothing, she returned to the other side of the room.

"No, it's a depressing view."

She called me.

"Come, there's nothing to see."

Without so much as the slightest preliminary caress, Jack Hold came over to Tatiana Karl.

Jack Hold possessed Tatiana Karl, ruthlessly. She offered no resistance, said nothing, refused no demand, marveled at the intensity of his passion.

Their pleasure was great, and mutual.

That moment when Lol was completely forgotten, that extended flash, in the unvarying time of her watchful wait, Lol wanted that moment to be, without harboring the slightest hope of perceiving it. It was.

Holding her in a tight embrace, Jack Hold could not bring himself to move away from Tatiana Karl. He talked to her. Tatiana Karl was not quite certain for whom the words which Jack Hold said to her were intended. She was under no illusion whatsoever that they were addressed to her, nor did she believe they were meant for some other woman who, that day, was absent, but thought rather that, through them, he was unburdening his heart. But why this rather than some other time? Tatiana sought the answer by thinking back on their affair.

"Tatiana, you're my life, my life, Tatiana."

That day, Tatiana listened to her lover's wild words, at first simply pleased and happy, as always, to be a vaguely defined woman in the arms of a man.

"Tatiana, I love you, I love you, Tatiana."

Tatiana acquiesced, in a comforting, maternally tender voice:

"Yes. I'm here. Here beside you."

At first simply pleased and happy, as always, to see how free someone could be with her, then, suddenly, taken aback by the pernicious intention of the words.

"Tatiana, my sister, Tatiana."

To hear that, to imagine what he might say if she were not Tatiana, ah! sweet words!

"How can I do even more to you, Tatiana?"

We must have been there for at least an hour now, all three of us, an hour since she had seen us appear in turn in the frame of the window, that mirror which reflected nothing and before which she must have shivered with delight to feel as excluded as she wished to be.

"Maybe, without realizing it . . ." Tatiana said, "maybe you and I . . ."

It was dark at last.

Again Jack Hold began, with ever increasing difficulty, to take Tatiana Karl. At one point, he spoke constantly to some other woman who could not see, who could not hear, and with whom, in intimate contact, he strangely seemed to find himself.

And then there came a time when Jack Hold no longer was able to take Tatiana Karl again.

Tatiana Karl thought that he had fallen asleep. She granted him this moment of respite, snuggled up against this person who was a thousand miles away, who was nowhere, in the fields, and waited until he would seize her again. But she waited in vain. As he lay sleeping, or so she thought, she spoke to him:

"Ah, those words, you shouldn't say them, they're dangerous."

Tatiana Karl was sorry. She was not the woman he might have learned to love. But why couldn't she be, why couldn't she be the one just as well as someone else? It was understood from the start that she would merely be his South Tahla mistress, that this would define the limits of their love, she did not want the sudden and overwhelming change in Michael Richardson to play any part in her affair. But now, suddenly, were these words of love wasted?

That evening, Tatiana says, for the first time since the Town Beach ball, she again discovered, she again savored the full sweetness of sentiment.

I went back to the window, she was still there, there in that field, alone in that field in a way she could never reveal to anyone. She told me, at the same time as I became aware of my love, of her inviolable self-sufficiency, a giantess with the hands of a child.

He went back to the bed, stretched out beside Tatiana Karl. They lay folded in each other's arms, bathed in the evening coolness. The sweet smell of ripe rye drifted in through the open window. He mentioned it to Tatiana.

"Can you smell the rye?"

She breathed in, she could smell it. She told him it was getting late and said that she had to go. She arranged to meet him three days later, fearing he would refuse. On the contrary, he agreed, without even checking to make sure he was free that day.

At the door, she asked him if he could give her any inkling as to his feelings.

"I want to see you again," he said, "to keep on seeing you again and again."

"You shouldn't talk like that," she said, "you really shouldn't."

After she was gone, I turned out the lights and waited, in order to give Lol a chance to leave the field and get back to town without any risk of running into me.

The following day I make arrangements to get away from the hospital for an hour in the afternoon. I go looking for her. I take a turn past the cinema in front of which she first found me. I drive past her house: the doors and windows of the living room are wide open, John Bedford's car is not there, it's Thursday, a school holiday, I can hear the laughter of a little girl coming from the lawn just outside the billiard room, then the mingled laughter of two little girls, she has only daughters, three of them. A maid with a white apron, young and rather pretty, comes out onto the steps, starts down a path toward the lawn, notices me parked in the street, smiles at me, and disappears. I drive off. I want to avoid going toward the Forest Hotel, I drive there anyway, stop the car and circle the hotel, keeping a good distance away as I do, I walk around the field of rye, the field is empty, she only comes when we're there, Tatiana and I. I leave. I drive slowly through the main streets of town, it occurs to me that she may be on one of the streets in Tatiana's neighborhood. There she is. She is walking along the boulevard which goes past Tatiana's house, about two hundred yards from the house. I park the car and follow her on foot. She walks all the way to the end of the boulevard. She is walking fairly fast, her gait easy and relaxed, a lovely sight to behold. She seems taller to me than on the other two occasions when I've seen her in the past. She is wearing her gray coat and a black, brimless hat. She turns right, into a street leading toward her own house, and disappears. Exhausted, I return to the car. So she's still taking her walks, and I can always manage a chance meeting if I can't bear to wait for our next scheduled date. She was walking rather fast, then at times she would slow down and stop, then off she would go again. She was taller than she had been in her house, taller and more slender. I recognized the gray coat, but not the black, brimless hat, she hadn't worn it in the rye field. I shall never accost her. Just as no

one else accosts her. I shall never go up to her and say:
"I couldn't wait for such and such a day, or such and
such a time." Tomorrow. Does she go out on Sunday?
Here it is Sunday. It is vast and beautiful. I'm not on
duty at the hospital. One day separates me from her.
For hours on end I go looking for her, in the car, on
foot. She is nowhere to be found. Her house is still the
same, with the bay windows open. John Bedford's car
is still not there, no little-girl laughter now. At five
o'clock I go to the Beugners for tea. Tatiana reminds
me of Lol's invitation for the day after tomorrow,
Monday. An awkward invitation. It's as though she
were trying to keep up with the Jonses, Tatiana says,
to act like a good middle-class housewife. This evening,
this Sunday evening, I drive past her house again. Her
house with the open bay windows. John Bedford's
violin. She is there, she is sitting in the living room.
Her hair is down. Three little girls move to and fro
around her, busy doing something, but what it is I
can't make out. She doesn't move, lost in her thoughts,
says nothing to the children, the children say nothing
to her. One by one—I remain there for a fairly long
time—the little girls give her a kiss and leave the room.
Lights go on up on the second story. She remains in the
living room, in the same position as before. Suddenly
she smiles to herself. I don't call out to her. She gets
up, turns out the lights, and disappears. It's tomorrow.

It's a tearoom, not far from the Green Town station.
Green Town is at least an hour by bus from South

Tahla. She's the one who picked the place, this tea-room.

She was already there when I arrived. There weren't many people, it's still early. I spotted her immediately, sitting by herself, surrounded by empty tables. From the other end of the room, she smiled at me, a pleased, conventional smile, different from any smile I had seen from her before.

She greeted me pleasantly, almost politely. But when she lifted her eyes, I saw them filled with a wild, crazy joy with which her whole being must have been inflamed: the joy of being there, across from him, across from the secret he implies, a secret she will never reveal, and he knows it.

"My God! how I've looked for you, I've tramped the streets looking for you."

"I'm a great walker," she said. "Did I forget to tell you? I go for long walks every day."

"You told Tatiana," I said.

Once again I have the feeling I can stop right there, be satisfied with no more than simply having her there to look at.

Merely seeing her unnerves me terribly. She makes no demands as far as conversation goes, and is capable of enduring silence indefinitely. I want to do something, say something, a long-drawn-out bellow made up of all words fused into one and reduced to the same magma, intelligible to Lol Stein. I say nothing. I say:

"I have never waited for anything the way I've waited for today, when nothing will happen."

"We're moving toward something. Even if nothing happens, we're moving toward some goal."

"What goal?"

"I don't know. The only thing I know anything about is the immobility of life. Therefore, when this immobility is destroyed, I know it."

She is again wearing the white dress she was wearing the first time I saw her at Tatiana Karl's. It is visible under her gray raincoat, which is unbuttoned. As I look at the dress, she takes off her raincoat, revealing her bare arms. Summer is in her cool arms.

Leaning toward me, she whispers:

"Tatiana."

I knew that she was asking me a question.

"We saw each other on Tuesday."

She knew that. She becomes beautiful, that same sort of beauty that, late at night four days before, I had snatched away from her.

She asks in a rush:

"How was it?"

I didn't answer immediately. She thought I hadn't understood the question. She goes on:

"How was Tatiana?"

If she hadn't mentioned Tatiana Karl, I would have done it myself. She is full of anxiety. She doesn't know herself what is going to ensue, what the reply is going to lead to. We are both face to face with the question, her admission.

I accept this. I already accepted it on Tuesday. And probably even from the very first moment I met her.

"Tatiana is admirable."

"You can't bear to be without her, can you?"

I see that a dream is almost realized. Flesh is being rent, is bleeding, is awakening. She is trying to listen to some inner commotion, fails to, is overwhelmed by the realization, however incomplete, of her desire. Her eyelids are fluttering from a light too strong. I avert my gaze for as long as it takes for that endless moment to pass.

I reply:

"I can't bear to be without her."

Then it's impossible, I look at her again. Her eyes are filled with tears. She is repressing some frightful pain to which she fails to yield, which, on the contrary, she cultivates with all her might, on the edge of bringing it to climactic expression, which probably would be akin to happiness. I say nothing. I offer her no help in dealing with this anomaly of her make-up. The moment is drawing to a close. Lol's tears are checked, returned to the controlled stream of her body's tears. The moment has moved neither toward victory nor toward defeat, has taken on no other coloring pleasure alone, a negative force, has passed.

She says:

"And you'll see, soon it will be even better between you and Tatiana."

I smile at her, still in the same state of being aware, and at the same time ignorant, of a future which she alone controls without knowing it.

There are two of us who don't know. I say:

"I hope so."

Her face changes, blanches.

"But what about us?" she says. "What will we do about that?"

I understand, I would have rendered this same verdict if I had been in her place. I can put myself in her place, but I would be doing so from a direction she would not approve of.

"I hope so too," she says.

She lowers her voice. Her eyelids are dotted with fine beads of perspiration whose taste I know from the other night.

"But you have Tatiana Karl, there's no one else like her in your life." *She puts words in his mouth*

I repeat:

"No one else like her in my life. When I talk about her, that's how I describe her." *Jack repeats & so believes*

"You must," she says, then adds: "I love you, you have no idea how much I love you already!"

The word travels through space, seeks, and alights. She has placed the word on me. *— word is flighty — but a construct*

She loves, loves the man who must love Tatiana. No one. No one loves Tatiana in me. I belong to a perspective which she is in the process of constructing with impressive obstinacy, I shall not resist. Tatiana, little by little, is forcing her way in, is breaking down the doors.

love in the △

Who? Lol?

"Come on, we're going for a walk. I have some things I want to tell you."

We walked down the boulevard behind the railroad station, which is almost deserted. I took her arm.

"Tatiana arrived at the room shortly after I did. Sometimes she does that on purpose to try and make me think she's not coming. I'm aware of that. But yesterday I had a terrible desire to have Tatiana there with me."

I wait. She asks no questions. How do I know that she knows? That she is sure I saw her out there in the field of rye? From this: from the fact that she is not asking any questions? I go on:

"When she did arrive, she had that holier-than-thou air about her, you know, that air of remorse and false shame, but you and I both know what that air conceals in Tatiana."

"Dear Tatiana."

"Yes."

He tells Lol Stein:

"Tatiana removes her clothes, and Jack Hold watches her, stares with interest at this woman who is not the woman he loves. As each article of clothing falls, he recognizes still more of this insatiable body to whose existence he is quite indifferent. He has already explored this body, he knows it better than does Tatiana herself. And yet his eyes remain fixed upon its hollows, where the skin is thin, of a white which subtly follows the lines of the body, shades either to a pure arterial blue or to a sunny brown. He stares at her until the identity of each line is blurred, and even the entire body."

But Tatiana is speaking:

"But Tatiana is saying something," Lol Stein murmurs.

To make her happy, I would invent God if I had to.

"She utters your name."

I did not invent that.

He hides Tatiana Karl's face beneath the sheets, and thus has her headless body at his disposal, at his entire disposal. He turns the body this way and that, raises it, does with it whatever he desires, spreads the limbs or draws them in close, stares fixedly at its irreversible beauty, enters it, remains motionless, awaits being trapped into forgetfulness, forgetfulness is there.

"Ah, how beautifully Tatiana knows how to let herself go, it's absolutely amazing, it must be extraordinary."

This rendezvous was a source of great pleasure to Tatiana and him alike, greater than usual.

"Doesn't she say anything else?"

"Beneath the sheet that covers her, she talks of Lol Stein."

Tatiana is going on in great detail, and frequently repeating the same details over and over again, about the ball at the municipal casino where, people say, Lol Stein went mad. She describes at great length the thin woman dressed in black, Anne-Marie Stretter, and the couple they formed, she and Michael Richardson, tells how they had the strength to keep on dancing, how absolutely amazing it was to see the way they had been able to retain that habit in the course of that wild night which seemed to have banished every other habit from their lives, even, Tatiana says, the habit of love.

"You have no idea," Lol says.

Once again I have to stop Tatiana from talking, there beneath the sheet. But then, much later, she starts in again. As she is leaving, she asks Jack Hold if he has seen Lol again. Although they had never agreed between them how to respond to such a question, he decides to lie.

Lol stops.

"Tatiana wouldn't understand," she says.

I lean forward, I smell the odor of her face. She is wearing some little-girl perfume, like talcum powder.

"Contrary to habit, I let her leave before me. Then I turned out the lights in the room. I stayed there in the dark for a long time."

She dodges the question by her reply, but only by a hair's breadth, just long enough to say something else —with a trace of sadness in her voice:

"Tatiana is always in such a hurry."

I reply:

"Yes."

Looking at the boulevard, she says:

"I have no way of knowing what went on in that room between Tatiana and you. I'll never know. When you tell me, it's something else."

She sets off walking again, then asks in a near whisper:

"Tatiana, with her head hidden beneath the sheet, she's not me, is she?"

I put my arm around her, I must be hurting her, she gives a little cry, I let her go.

"It's for you."

We're hidden below a wall. I can feel her breath against my chest. I can no longer see her face, her sweet face, its diaphanous outline, her eyes almost always filled with surprise, her searching, astonished eyes.

And it is at this point that the idea of her absence became unbearable to me. I told her so, said that the thought of leaving her was sheer torture to me. She, Lol, had no such feeling, she was surprised by my words. She did not understand.

Why should I leave?

I said I was sorry. But there's nothing I can do about the feeling of horror, it's still there. I am aware of her absence, her absence yesterday, even now I miss her constantly.

She has talked to her husband. She has told him she felt things were practically over between them. He didn't believe her. Wasn't it a fact that she had already told him such things in the past? No, she never had.

I ask: has she always returned home?

I said it casually enough, but she was not fooled by the sudden change in my voice. She says:

"Lol has always returned home safe and sound with John Bedford."

Then she goes off on a long tangent about a fear of hers: those close to her, especially her husband, believe that it is not impossible that she might fall ill again one day. This is why she hasn't spoken too him as candidly as she would have liked. I refrain from asking her what basis there is at present for this fear. She doesn't offer any explanation. In all probability she hasn't once alluded to this threat in ten years.

"John Bedford is under the impression he saved me from the depths of despair. I never disabused him of that notion, I've never told him it was something else."

"What?"

"That from the first moment that woman walked into the room, I ceased to love my fiancé."

We are sitting on a bench. Lol has missed the train she had made up her mind to take back. I kiss her, she returns my kisses.

"When I say that I no longer loved him, I mean to

say that you have no idea to what lengths one can go in the absence of love."

"Give me some idea."

"I can't."

"Tatiana's life means no more to me than the life of some stranger, some distant person whose name I don't even know."

"It's even more than that."

We remain in each other's arms. I have her on my lips, warm on my lips.

"It's a substitute."

I don't let her go. She is talking to me. Trains are passing.

"You wanted to see them?"

I take her mouth. I reassure her. But she wrests free, stares at the ground.

"Yes. I wasn't there any longer. They took me with them. When I woke up, they were gone."

She frowns slightly, and this is so unlike her, I know, that I'm alarmed by it.

"Sometimes I'm a little frightened it might start all over again."

I don't take her in my arms again.

"No."

"But we're not afraid. That's only a word."

She sighs.

"I don't understand who's there in my place."

I bring her closer to me. Her lips are cool, almost cold.

"Don't ever change."

"But what if someday I . . .?" she stumbles over

the word she fails to find. "Will they still let me take my walks?"

"I'll hide you."

"If that day comes, will they be mistaken?"

"No."

She turns around and says, with a smile which bespeaks a staggering confidence:

"I know that whatever I do, you'll understand. The problem will be proving to the others you're right."

At that moment, I am ready to take her away with me forever. She nestles against me, ready to be taken away.

"I want to stay with you."

"Why don't you?"

"Tatiana."

"You've got a point."

"You might just as well love Tatiana," she says, "it wouldn't change anything for . . ."

She adds:

"I don't understand what's happening."

"It wouldn't change anything."

I ask:

"Why this dinner day after tomorrow?"

"I must, for Tatiana. Quiet, let's not say a word for a moment."

Her silence. We remain motionless, our faces scarcely touching, without a word, for a long time. The noise of the trains merges into a single outcry, which reaches our ears. Without moving, her lips all but closed, she says to me:

"In a certain state of mind, all trace of feeling is

banished. Whenever I remain silent in a certain way, I don't love you, have you noticed that?"

"Yes, I've noticed."

She stretches, laughs.

"And then I begin to breathe again," she says.

I'm supposed to see Tatiana again on Thursday at five o'clock. I tell her so.

Thus this dinner at Lol's took place.

Three other people, whom neither Peter Beugner nor I had met, are invited. An elderly lady—a professor at the Uxbridge Conservatory of Music—and her two children, a young man and a woman whose husband, whom John Bedford is apparently anxious to meet, is not scheduled to arrive until after dinner.

I am the last to arrive.

I have not arranged any further meeting with her. As she was about to board her train, she told me that we would set a date tonight. I'm waiting.

Over dinner, the conversation drags. Lol does nothing to enliven it, perhaps she is not even aware of the heavy silence. Nor does she give us any hint, however slight, of the reason why she has brought us together this evening. Why? For the simple reason that we are probably the only people she knows well enough to invite to her house. If, as Tatiana says, John Bedford has some friends, especially musician friends, she also tells me that he sees them without his wife, outside his home. It's obvious that Lol has brought together everyone she knows. But why?

A private conversation is developing between the elderly lady and John Bedford. I hear: "If only the young people were aware of the existence of our concerts, believe me, we'd have full houses." The young woman is talking to Peter Beugner. I hear: "Paris in October." Then: "I've finally made up my mind."

Again, Tatiana Karl, Lol Stein, and I find ourselves together: none of us says a word. Tatiana phoned me last night: Yesterday I went looking for Lol, without finding her either in town or at her house. The living room, where she and her daughters can usually be seen after dinner, was dark. I slept badly, still obsessed by this same doubt that daylight alone can dispel: that someone may notice something, that she may no longer be allowed out alone in South Tahla.

Tatiana seems impatient for the meal to end, she is

nervous and worried. I have a feeling she would like to ask Lol something.

Between us, words are few and far between. Tatiana asks Lol where she intends to spend her vacation. In France, Lol says. Again we fall silent. Tatiana studies both of us in turn, she must realize that the interest we showed in each other, Lol and I, the other evening, is missing. Since our previous assignation at the Forest Hotel—as a bachelor I'm often invited to the Beugners for dinner—she has not spoken of Lol again.

Little by little, everyone around the table enters into the conversation. People are asking the hostess questions. The three guests from out of town seem to be on a footing of affectionate familiarity with her. People are a shade more solicitous with her than they need be, than their remarks or replies require. In everyone's gentle amiability—which is also the attitude of her husband when dealing with her—I detect the sign of the anxiety, both past and present, which is the constant concern of those around her. They speak to her because it would be awkward not to, but they are afraid of what she may reply. Is their concern more noticeable tonight than usual? I don't know. If not, I find that reassuring, I find in that fact the confirmation of what Lol has told me about her husband: John Bedford suspects no one or nothing, his sole concern being, so it would seem, to prevent his wife from saying something she shouldn't, something dangerous, in public. Tonight especially, perhaps. He has misgivings about this dinner party which, in spite of his feelings, he has allowed Lol to give. If there is someone he fears, it is Tatiana Karl, the way Tatiana stares insistently at his wife, that I know, I have watched him closely, and he has noticed this. Even when he is engrossed in his conversations with the elderly lady about his concerts, he does not fail to keep an eye on Lol. He loves Lol. But, if he were to lose Lol, is it probable he would be just the same? just as affable? The attraction—how strange this is—that Lol exerts on both of us might sour my present relationship with him. I don't believe he knows her except through the second-hand reports about her past insanity, he must think he has a wife full of unexpected charms, not the least of which is that of her being threatened. He thinks he is protecting his wife.

Between courses while the obvious absurdity of Lol's attempt at a party hovers, like some sterilizing agent, above us, my love revealed itself, I felt it become visible and observed, despite myself, by Tatiana Karl. But still Tatiana has doubts.

The people at the table were talking about the house the Bedfords had formerly lived in, of the grounds around it.

Lol is to my right, between Peter Beugner and me. Suddenly she leans over toward me, close to me, her eyes not fixed upon me, with no expression on her face, as though she were about to ask me a question which sticks in her throat. And it is from this position, almost touching me, that she asks the woman on the other side of the table:

"Are there any children in the park?"

I knew she was there on my right, one of her hands was all that separated me from her face, a hand risen from out of my vague impressions of the whole scene, suddenly a sharp point, a fixed point, of love. It is then that the rhythm of my breathing broke, is stifled by too much air. Tatiana noticed it. So did Lol. She leaned away, very slowly. The lie was again covered over. Again I gained control of myself, and was calm. Tatiana no doubt vacillates between the thought that this gesture stemmed from Lol's innate absent-mindedness and the thought that it was not entirely inadvertent, though she has no idea what it means. The lady noticed nothing, she answers:

"There are some new children in the park. They're little terrors."

"And what about the little shrubs I planted before I left?"

"I'm afraid, Lol . . ."

Lol evinces surprise. She is hoping for some interruption in the endless repetition of her life.

"One ought to destroy a house after one leaves it. There are people who do, you know."

With subtle irony, the lady reminds Lol that other people might have need of the houses one left behind. Lol begins to laugh and laugh. An infectious laugh, which first set me, then Tatiana, to laughing too.

These grounds where her daughters grew up seem to have occupied her greatly during the ten years of her life she lived there. She left them in perfect condition for the new proprietors. Her musician friends mention the trees and the flower beds as being especially worthy of praise. Lol was granted those grounds for ten years so that she could be here tonight, miraculously preserved by her difference from those who gave it to her.

Doesn't she miss that house? the young woman asks,

that big, beautiful house in Uxbridge? For a moment
Lol doesn't answer, all eyes are upon her, something, a
sort of shudder, passes across her eyes. She freezes because of something going on inside her, what? unknown, savage leitmotifs, wild birds in her life—how
can we tell?—which wing through her from side to
side, and are swallowed up? and then, after they are
gone, the wind caused by their passage subsides? She
says that she doesn't remember ever having lived there.
The sentence remains unfinished. Two seconds pass,
she regains control of herself, says with a laugh that she
is only joking, that what she is trying to say is that she is
happier here in South Tahla than she was in Uxbridge.
No one picks her up on it, she enunciates clearly:
South Tahla, Uxbridge. She laughs a little too long,
offers a few too many explanations. I'm suffering, but
only slightly, everyone is afraid, but only a trifle. Lol
falls silent. Tatiana is probably convinced about her
theory concerning Lol's absent-mindedness. Lol Stein
is still ill.

We leave the table.

The young woman's husband arrives with two
friends. He is carrying on the musical evenings in Uxbridge that John Bedford had started. They have not
seen each other for some time, they are talking with
great gusto and obvious pleasure. Time ceases to weigh
heavily, there are enough of us now so that people can
move to and fro from group to group without anyone
noticing it—anyone, that is, except Tatiana Karl.

Perhaps Lol's bringing us together tonight was not
inadvertent, perhaps she has done it in order to see the

two of us together, Tatiana and I, to see what has become of our relationship since she burst into my life. I don't know.

As Tatiana gives her a big hug, Lol finds herself trapped. I think of the night when John Bedford first met her: Tatiana, as she carries on a conversation with her, is blocking her passage in such a clever manner that Lol fails to realize that she cannot get past, that Tatiana is preventing her from moving on to her other guests, she draws her away from the group she was with, takes her away with her, isolates her. This maneuver takes Tatiana all of twenty minutes. Lol seems relaxed there at the far end of the living room, seated with Tatiana at a small table between the outside steps and the bay window through which, the other evening, I watched them.

This evening they are both wearing dark dresses which make them seem taller and more slender and, to a man's eyes perhaps, less obviously different one from the other. Tatiana, in contrast to the way she wears her hair for her lovers, tonight has swept it back into a thick, heavy knot which reaches almost to her shoulders. Her dress, unlike her tight-fitting, severe afternoon suits, is not snug. Lol's dress, in contrast to Tatiana's, I believe, is close-fitting and makes her look even more like some slightly stiff, well-behaved, grownup schoolgirl. Her hair, as usual, is drawn back into a tight chignon just above the nape of her neck; for ten years, perhaps, she has worn it in this way. Tonight she is wearing make-up which is a little too heavy, it seems to me, and carelessly applied.

Tatiana's smile whenever she manages to have Lol

to herself is recognizable now. She is waiting for the secret to be revealed, she hopes it will be new, touching, not completely true, but a lie awkward enough so that she, Tatiana, will be able to see through it to the truth.

Seeing them thus together there, one could easily believe that Tatiana Karl is the only person beside myself who is not in the least concerned about the oddities, latent or overt, of Lol's behavior.

I approach their little island. Tatiana still doesn't see me.

I understood the sense of the question she was asking Lol from the movement of her lips. I saw her form the word "happiness."

"Your happiness? What about this happiness of yours?"

Lol smiles in my direction. Come. She allows me time enough to move closer. I am at an oblique angle to Tatiana, who has eyes only for Lol. I walk over silently, slipping past the other guests. I am close enough now so that I can hear. I stop. Still, Lol does not yet answer. She raises her eyes to me, to let Tatiana know of my presence. She knows. Her reaction is one of obvious irritation, which she quickly represses: she wants to see me at the Forest Hotel, not here with Lol.

Seen from a distance, all three of us seem nonchalant.

Tatiana and I are waiting anxiously for Lol's reply. My heart is beating wildly, and I'm afraid Tatiana may detect—only she can—this chaotic pounding of her lover's blood. I'm so close to her I almost touch her. I take a step back. She noticed nothing.

Lol is about to reply. I am ready for anything. Ready for her to finish me off in the same way she discovered me. She answers. My heart slows down and almost stops.

"My happiness is here."

Slowly, Tatiana turns around to me and, smiling with remarkable self-possession, calls upon me to concur with her own opinion about the way Lol's statement has been phrased.

"How beautifully she says that. Did you hear her?"

"She does indeed."

"But really so beautifully, don't you agree?"

Then Tatiana casts an eye around the room, at the noisy knot of people at the other end of the living room, those outward and visible signs of Lol's existence.

"I've been thinking about you a great deal since I last saw you."

With a childish movement, Lol's eyes follow Tatiana's gaze about the room. She doesn't understand. Tatiana's tone is both sententious and tender.

"But what about John," she says, "and your daughters? What are you going to do with them?"

Lol laughs.

"You were looking at them, so that's what you were looking at!"

She can't stop laughing. At length Tatiana is compelled to join in too, but her laughter is tinged with pain, she has lost her social grace, I recognize the woman who telephones me during the night.

"You frighten me, Lol."

Lol is surprised. Her surprise strikes a direct blow at

the fear which Tatiana refuses to admit. She has detected the lie. It is done. Gravely, she asks:

"What are you afraid of, Tatiana?"

Suddenly Tatiana is no longer hiding anything. But without revealing the real source of her fear.

"I don't know."

Again Lol's gaze surveys the room, and she explains to Tatiana something other than what she wanted to learn. She begins talking again, and this time Tatiana is caught in her own trap, having asked about Lol Stein's happiness.

"But I didn't want anything, Tatiana, do you understand, I didn't want any part of all the things that are happening, that now exist. None of it makes any sense.

"And if you had wanted it, would it have made any difference now?"

Lol stops to reflect, and her thoughtful air, her air of pretending that she has forgotten, has the perfection of a work of art. I know that she has said the first thing that came to mind:

"It would have been the same. It was the same as now from the very first day. For me."

Tatiana gives a sigh, a long sigh, moans, moans, on the verge of tears.

"But what about this happiness, tell me about this happiness, please, just a word or two about it!"

I say:

"Lol Stein probably had it within her when she encountered it."

With the same slow movement as before, Tatiana turns again to me. I pale. The curtain has just risen on the pain Tatiana is suffering. But, strangely, her suspicions are not immediately directed at Lol.

"How do you know such things about Lol?"

She means: how do you know such things when a woman doesn't? another woman who could be Lol Stein?

Tatiana's dry, stinging tone is the same one she sometimes uses at the Forest Hotel. Lol is sitting straight in her chair. Why this terror? She makes a move as though to flee, she is going to leave us both there.

"You can't talk like that, you just can't."

"I'm sorry," Tatiana says. "Jack Hold has been in a strange state for the past few days. He says anything that comes into his mind."

She asked me on the telephone whether I thought there were any possible way, not for us to be in love, but for there to be some amatory relationship between us at some future time, some time far in the future.

"Can you act as though it were not completely out of the question that some day, by working at it, you might find something new about me: I'll change my way of talking, buy a whole new wardrobe, I'll cut my hair, nothing will be the same."

I stood my ground, stuck to what I had always maintained. I told her I loved her. She hung up.

Lol is reassured. Again Tatiana begs her:

"Tell me something about your happiness, please do."

Lol asks, in a friendly way, with no show of irritation or annoyance:

"Why, Tatiana?"

"What a question, Lol!"

Then Lol searches, her face grows tense, and, with some difficulty, she tries to say something about this happiness.

"The other evening, it was at dusk, but long after the sun had gone down, for some reason there was a brief moment when it grew lighter outdoors, I don't know why, it lasted a minute. I didn't actually look at the ocean. I saw it reflected in a mirror on the wall in front of me. I had a strong urge to go there, to go and see it."

She doesn't go on. I ask:

"And did you?"

Lol's reaction to that question is immediate.

"No. I'm sure I didn't, I didn't go down to the beach. The reflection in the mirror was there."

Tatiana has forgotten me for Lol. She takes her hand and kisses it.

"Tell me more, Lol."

"I didn't go down to the beach, I . . ." Lol says.

Tatiana does not press her further.

Yesterday Lol took a quick trip to the shore, that's why I couldn't find her. She failed to mention it. Suddenly, like a slap, the image of the field of rye comes back to me, I ask myself, and the question is sheer torture, I ask myself what I may expect next from Lol. What? Am I, is it possible I could be, taken in by her madness? What did she go looking for at the seashore, where I am not, what sustenance? so far from me? If Tatiana doesn't ask the question, I'm going to. Tatiana asks it.

"Where did you go? Do you mind telling us?"

Lol says, and I seem to detect a slight trace of regret that her answer is made to Tatiana, or perhaps I am mistaken again:

"To Town Beach."

John Bedford, doubtless with the thought in mind of breaking up our group, puts on some records. I don't stop to think, I don't even ask myself whether I should, nor do I stop to consider what would be the best thing to do, I invite Lol to dance. We move away from Tatiana, who remains alone.

I dance too slowly, and often my feet are two lead weights, I can't keep time to the music. Lol absently follows my mistakes.

Tatiana's eyes pursue us on our painful course around the living room.

Finally, Peter Beugner makes his way over to her and invites her to dance.

I've had Lol in my arms for a hundred years. I talk to her in such a way that my words are indiscernible. Thanks to Peter Beugner's maneuvers on the floor as he dances, Tatiana is hidden from us. In our hiding place, she can neither see us nor hear us.

"You went to the seashore."

"Yesterday I went down to Town Beach."

"Why didn't you say anything about going? Why? Why did you go there?"

"I thought that . . . "

She fails to finish the sentence. I press her gently.

"Try to tell me. That . . ."

"You've probably already guessed."

"This can't go on. I must see you, this can't go on."

Here's Tatiana. Has she noticed that I have just said something, then repeated it in a rush? Lol and I say nothing. Then, once again, we are in the line of vision of John Bedford, whose tepid, only slightly intrigued gaze is upon us.

Though still in my arms, Lol has lost the beat and stopped following me, a dead weight all of a sudden.

"We can go to Town Beach together if you like, the day after tomorrow."

"For how long?"

"For a day, maybe."

We agree to meet at the station very early in the morning. She specifies a time. I have to speak to Peter Beugner and let him know I'll be away for a day. Shall I do it?

I invent:

Look, they've stopped talking again, Tatiana is thinking. I'm used to it, I know how to make him moody, silent and depressed, he has trouble getting out of these states, he seems to enjoy them. But I don't think I've ever seen him as silent with me as he is now with Lol Stein, even when he came for me the first time, one afternoon when Peter was away, and drove me to the Forest Hotel, without ever saying a word. Here is what I don't know: that man who is fading away, who says that he loves, desires, wants to see her again, who fades away even more as he says this. I must be slightly feverish tonight. Everything is leaving me, my life, my life.

Again, like a good girl, Lol is dancing, following me. When Tatiana cannot see, I move Lol away from me so that I can see her eyes. I see them: a transparency is looking at me. Again I cannot see. I pull her back against me, she does not resist; no one, I believe, is paying any attention to us. The transparency has gone through me, I can still see it, blurred now, it has moved on toward something else that is less clear, something endless, it will move on toward something else, some endless thing that I will never know.

"Lol Stein, eh?"

"Ah, yes."

I hurt her. I thought so because I felt a warm "ah" against my neck.

"We must put an end to this. When?"

She does not reply. Tatiana is looking at us again.

I invent:

Tatiana is speaking to Peter Beugner:

"I must have a word with Jack Hold about Lol."

Is Peter Beugner mistaken concerning her true intention? His love for Tatiana is one that has survived more than one test, a sentiment which hangs heavily on him but which he will drag with him to the grave, they are united, their house is more solid than most, it has stood up beneath the buffeting of many a storm. In Tatiana's life, the one and only compelling and overriding obligation, which it is unthinkable she will ever give up some day, is the certainty that she will always come back to Peter Beugner, he is her return, her respite, her sole constancy.

I invent:

This evening, Peter Beugner, his ear to the wall, detects the slight crack in his wife's voice that she, Lol, always hears.

It is I who am responsible for the intimacy between them now, without either one of them ever acknowledging it.

Peter Beugner says:

"Lol Stein still isn't well. You saw how she was at dinner, how her mind wandered, it was really quite impressive, I'm sure that's what interests Jack Hold about her."

"Do you really think so? But isn't she playing on that interest?"

Peter Beugner's words are consoling:

"The poor girl, how could she?"

Peter Beugner takes his wife in his arms, he wants to prevent what he senses are the first pangs of suffering in her from developing. He says:

"Personally, I haven't noticed anything between them, absolutely nothing, I must say, except for that interest I mentioned to you."

Tatiana grows slightly impatient, but does not show it.

"I suggest you study them a little more closely."

"All right, I will."

Another record replaces the first. The couples have not separated. They are at the other end of the living room. The remarkable thing about them, suddenly, is not their awkwardness, which now is not all that noticeable, but the expression on their faces as they dance, an expression that is neither friendly nor polite nor bored but is rather—Tatiana is right—the mark of the absolutely rigid, stifling reserve that each of them exhibits toward the other. Especially when Jack Hold speaks to Lol and she answers him without there being the least change in this reserve, without it being possible for anyone to guess either the nature of the question asked or that of the answer which will be given.

Lol answers me:

"If only we knew when."

I forgot Tatiana Karl, I admit having committed that crime. I was in the train, I had her next to me for hours, we were already on our way to Town Beach.

"What's the point of taking this trip now?"

"It's summer. It's the best time."

Since I don't answer her, she goes on to explain:

"And besides, we haven't any time to lose. Tatiana's beginning to fall in love with you. . . ."

She stops. Is it conceivable that Lol would like to have happen between Peter Beugner and Tatiana what I merely imagine in my mind?

"Is that what you wanted?"

"Yes. But you were supposed to fall in love with her too. She wasn't supposed to know anything about it."

Her air of apparent sophistication might have reassured observers less demanding than Tatiana and Peter Beugner.

"I may be wrong. Everything may be perfectly all right."

"But why did she go to Town Beach again?"

"For me."

Peter Beugner is smiling at me cordially. Lurking behind that smile there is now a conviction, a warning, that if tomorrow finds Tatiana in tears, I shall be dismissed from his section at the hospital. I imagine in my mind that Peter Beugner is lying.

"You're making a mountain out of a mole hill," he says to his wife. "He couldn't care less about Lol Stein. He scarcely listens to what she says."

Tatiana Karl finds herself surrounded by lies, she has a moment of dizziness, and the thought of her death flows in upon her, cool water which she rubs upon that burn, let it come and cover over that shame, let it come, and then the truth will be known. What truth? Tatiana gives a sigh. The dance is over.

I danced with the woman from Uxbridge, danced well in fact, and I talked with her, I committed that crime as well, and I was relieved to commit it. And Tatiana must have been convinced that it was Lol Stein. But did I discover what intrigues me about Lol Stein on my own, wasn't it she who showed it to me, isn't it something of hers? The only thing new for Tatiana, betrayed tonight, the only new development for her in years, is the fact that she is suffering. I imagine to myself that this new development twists her heart, makes her start to perspire heavily at the roots of her sumptuous head of hair, strips her expression of its haughty desolation, diminishes it, threatens to totter her perennial pessimism: who knows? perhaps the white standard of lovers on their maiden voyage will pass close by my house?

Tatiana makes her way through the dancers, reaches my side, asks me for this dance, which is just starting.

I dance with Tatiana Karl.

Lol is seated next to the record player. She is the only person who does not seem to have noticed. She is glancing absently through a stack of records, she seems depressed. This is what I think about Lol Stein tonight: things are becoming somewhat clearer around her, and she is suddenly seeing the sharp edges, the remains that are left here and there throughout the world, which turn this way and that, she sees this left-over already half eaten by rats, Tatiana's pain, and is embarrassed by it, sentiment is rife everywhere, people are slipping on that greasy substance. She used to think that it was possible for there to be a time which filled and emptied alternately, which filled and emptied, and then was ready to be used again, always, to be used and reused, she still believes it, she will always believe it, she will never be cured.

In urgent, whispered tones, Tatiana is talking to me about Lol.

"When Lol speaks of happiness, what does she mean?"

I didn't lie.

"I don't know."

"What in the world's wrong with you, what's wrong with you?"

For the first time since the beginning of her affair with Jack Hold, Tatiana, with a show of indecency, with her husband looking on, lifts her face toward her lover, till it is so close to him that he could have placed his lips on her eyes. I say:

"I love you."

Once the words have been uttered, my mouth remained opened, so that they could flow out to the last drop. But, if the order is given once again, we shall have to do it all over again. Tatiana has seen that his eyes, beneath his lowered eyelids, were more than ever glancing in another direction, away from her, over there where the frail hands of Lol Stein are upon the pile of records.

This morning, over the phone, I had already told her.

She quivers at the insult, but the blow has been struck, Tatiana is felled. She accepts these words whenever she comes across them, Tatiana Karl does, today she rebels against them, but the fact remains she did hear them.

"Liar, liar."

She bows her head.

"I can't bring myself to look into your eyes any more, your filthy eyes!"

And then:

"It's because you believe, as far as what we do together is concerned, that that's of no importance, right?"

"No. It's because it's true. I love you."

"Shut up!"

She gathers her forces, tries to strike deeper, thrust harder.

"Have you noticed the way she is, how dead her body seems compared to mine, how unexpressive it is?"

"Yes, I've noticed."

"Have you noticed anything else about her you'd care to tell me?"

Lol is still over there by herself, going through the stack of records in her hands.

"It's not easy. Lol Stein is not, so to speak, anyone of any consequence."

In a voice that seems almost relieved, an almost bantering tone, Tatiana voices a threat the extent of which
she does not seem to appreciate but which I find ter-
rifying beyond description.

"I trust you realize that if you were to change too
much in your feelings toward me, I should have to stop
seeing you."

After that dance, I went over to Peter Beugner and
informed him of my intention to be away for the entire
day the day after tomorrow. He did not ask me where I
was going.

And then I came back over to Tatiana. I said to
her:

"I'll meet you tomorrow at six o'clock. At the hotel."

She said:

"No."

I am there at six o'clock on the appointed day. Tatiana probably will not come.

The gray shape is in the field of rye. I remain at the window for a long time. She does not move. I have the feeling she is fast asleep.

I stretch out on the bed. An hour goes by. When it grows dark, I turn on the lights.

I get up, I undress, I lie down again. I want Tatiana so badly I can't bear it. I want her so badly it makes me cry.

I don't know what to do. I go to the window, yes, she's fast asleep. She comes there to sleep. I leave the window, again I stretch out on the bed. I caress myself. He speaks to Lol Stein, lost forever, he comforts her for a nonexistent misfortune of which she is unaware. In this way he kills time. The moment of oblivion arrives. He calls out to Tatiana, asks her to help him.

Tatiana came in, her hair down, her eyes red too. Lol is immersed in her happiness, our sadness which sustains it seems negligible to me. The odor of the field drifts in through the window. And then Tatiana's drowns it out.

She sits down on the edge of the bed, and then slowly undresses, lies down beside me. She is crying. I say to her:

"I know how you feel, because I feel just as terrible."

I don't even try to take her, I know that I won't be able to. My love for that shape out there in the field is too great, will henceforth be too strong, it's all over.

"You came too late."

She buries her face in the sheets, speaks to me across a great distance.

"When?"

I can't resort to any more lies. I stroke her hair, which has spilled out over the bedclothes.

"This year, this summer, you came too late."

"I couldn't get here at the right time. It's because I started to love you too late."

She sits up, raises her head.

"Is it Lol?"

"I don't know."

More tears.

"Is it our dear little Lol?"

"Go, go on home."

"That lunatic?"

She is shouting. I stop her, with my hand over her mouth.

"Tell me it's Lol or I'll scream."

I lie for the last time.

"No. It's not Lol."

She gets up, paces back and forth across the room, stark naked, goes to the window, comes back, returns to the window, she too does not know what to do with herself, she has something on her mind, she hesitates, something she can't quite bring herself to say, then finally it comes out in a near whisper, almost a whisper. She tells me:

"We're not going to see each other any more. It's all over."

"I know."

Tatiana's ashamed of what will happen during the next few days and buries her face in her hands.

"Our little Lola, I know it's because of her."

Again anger seizes hold of her, snatches her from her tender daydream.

"How is it possible? a lunatic?"

"It's not Lol."

Calmer still, more controlled, she is trembling like a leaf. She comes over next to me. Her eyes are blinding mine.

"I'll find out, you know."

She moves away, she is facing the field of rye, and I can no longer see her face, which is turned toward the field, then I can see it again, the expression is still the same. She was watching the setting sun, the field of rye full of fire.

"I have ways of finding out, and when I do I'll warn her, oh, I'll do it gently, I won't hurt her, I'll know how to tell her to leave you alone. She's crazy, she won't even suffer when I tell her, that's how insane people are, you know."

"Friday at six o'clock, Tatiana, you'll come one more time."

She is crying. The tears are still flowing, from afar, from behind the tears, expected like all tears, arrived at last, and, I seem to recall, Tatiana appeared not to be displeased, seemed to be restored by them.

Like the first time, Lol is already there on the station platform, almost alone, the workers' trains are earlier, the cool wind slips in beneath her gray coat, her shadow is lengthened on the stone of the platform, stretching toward the shadows of the morning, it is mingled with a green light that shifts back and forth and catches on everything in myriads of little blinding explosions, fastens upon her eyes which, from a distance, are laughing as they come forward to meet me, the mineral light in them gleams, gleams bright and clear.

She is not hurrying, it is still five minutes to train time, her hair is slightly mussed, she is wearing no hat, to get here she had to walk through gardens, gardens where the wind blows free.

From up close, I recognize in the mineral glint of her eyes the joy of Lol Stein's entire being. She is steeped in joy, the signs of which are lighted to the very limits of possibility, they emanate from her entire being in waves. Strictly speaking, there is here present only the cause of that joy, for joy itself remains invisible.

The minute I saw her in her gray coat, in her South Tahla costume, she was the woman in the rye field behind the Forest Hotel. The woman who is not. And the woman who is, in that field and here beside me, I had them both, both enclosed within me.

The rest I forgot.

And all day long during the trip this situation remained unchanged, she was beside me and separated from me by a great distance, abyss and sister. Since I know—have I ever been so completely convinced of anything?—that I can never really know her, it is impossible for anyone to be closer to another human being than I am to her, closer to her than she is to herself, she who so constantly takes wing away from her living life. If there are others who come after me who know her as well, I will accept their coming.

We kill time, exchanging no word, stretching our

legs along the station platform. The moment our eyes meet, we burst out laughing.

Our train is virtually empty, a local train sandwiched in between the early morning workers' trains and the later commuters' trains. She has chosen it on purpose, she says, for the very reason that it is so slow. We will be in Town Beach around noon.

"I wanted to see Town Beach with you again."

"You've already seen it again, the day before yesterday."

Did she consider it unimportant whether she said it or not?

"No, I never really went back, not all the way back. The day before yesterday I didn't leave the station. I stayed in the waiting room. I fell asleep. I realized that without you there was no point in going. I wouldn't have recognized anything. I took the first train I could find back."

Gently, modestly, she leaned back against me. She was asking to be kissed, without openly asking.

"Whenever I remember Town Beach, I can't bear to think of it without you any more."

I put my arm around her waist and caressed her. The compartment is empty, like a bed that is made. Little girls, three little girls, crossed my mind. I don't know them. The oldest one, Tatiana says, is the image of Lol.

"Tatiana," she whispers.

"Tatiana was there yesterday. You were right. Admirable Tatiana."

Tatiana is there, like another person, Tatiana, mired within us, the Tatiana of yesterday and the one of tomorrow, whoever she may be. I plunge myself deep into her warm and muzzled body, an idle hour for Lol, the resplendent hour of her oblivion, I graft myself upon her, I pump Tatiana's blood. Tatiana is there, so that I can forget Lol Stein in her. She slowly becomes bloodless beneath me.

In the evening breeze, the rye rustles round the body of that woman who is keeping watch on a hotel where I am with someone else, with Tatiana.

Lol, close beside me, moves even closer, closer to Tatiana. The way she would like to. As the train stops at the various stations, the compartment remains empty. We are still alone in it.

"You want me to take you to a hotel after we get there?"

"I don't think so. I did want you to. But I don't any more."

This is all she has to say. She takes my hands, which I had withdrawn, and places them on her body again. I say, I beg:

"I can't bear it, I must see you every day."

"I can't bear it either. But we have to be careful. Two days ago I came home late. I found John out in the street, he was waiting for me."

A moment of doubt: did she see me at the window that last time, and the time before that? Did she see that I saw her? She mentions the incident quite casually. I don't ask her where she was coming from. She tells me.

"Sometimes I go out rather late. That night was one of those times."

"And did you do it again?"

"Yes. But that time he wasn't waiting for me. But that makes it all the more serious. Anyway, as far as our seeing each other every day, it's out of the question, because of Tatiana."

She snuggles up against me again, closes her eyes, is silent, attentively silent. She is the picture of contentment beside me. My eyes, my hands can detect nothing in any way out of the ordinary about her. Not the slightest trace of any difference. And yet, and yet. Who is there now, so near and yet so far, what marauding thoughts and ideas prowl through her mind, again and again, by day, by night, in every light? even right this minute? At this very moment when, holding her in my arms in this train, I might be tempted to think she was no different from any other woman? Around us, the walls: I try to scale them, catch hold, slip back, start over again, perhaps, perhaps, but my reason remains the same, undismayed, and I fall.

"I want to try and tell you something about this happiness I feel by loving you," she says. "I've been wanting to tell you for several days."

The sunlight coming through the train window falls on her. Her moving fingers punctuate her sentence, then settle back down on her white skirt. I cannot see her face.

"I don't love you and yet I do. You know what I mean."

I ask:

"Why don't you kill yourself? Why haven't you already killed yourself?"

"No, you're wrong, that's not it at all."

She says that to me without any trace of sadness. If

I'm wrong, I'm less wide of the mark than the others. I can only be wildly wrong about her. She knows it. She says:

"It's the first time you've been wrong."

"Are you glad?"

"Yes. Especially in that way. You are so close to . . . "

She tells me how happy, how concretely happy she is because she's in love. In her day-to-day existence with a man other than me, this happiness can coexist without creating the slightest problem.

When will it all end, in a few hours or in a few days? It won't be long before they take her back. They will comfort and console her, surround her with affection in her house in South Tahla.

"I'm not telling you the whole truth, I admit. At night I dream of telling you. But when morning comes, the urgency is less great. I understand."

"You mustn't tell me everything."

"You're right, I shouldn't. See, I'm not lying."

For the past three nights, ever since her trip to Town Beach, I've been dreading another trip she might take. The fear was still with me in the morning. I haven't told her that I've followed her when she goes out on her walks, that I drive past her house every day.

"There are times during the day when I manage to picture what it would be like without you, I still know you, but you've disappeared, you're no longer there. I don't do anything rash, I go out walking, I sleep, sleep very well in fact. I feel good without you since I've known you. Maybe it's at times like these, when I manage to convince myself that you're gone, that . . . "

I wait. When she really tries, she manages to continue. She is really trying. Her closed eyelids flutter imperceptibly, in time to the beating of her heart: she is calm, today she enjoys talking.

" . . . that I'm better, the woman I ought to be."

"And when would the suffering begin again?"

She is surprised.

"But . . . it wouldn't."

"Hasn't it ever happened to you?"

Her tone is different, she is hiding something.

"You see, that's odd, isn't it. I don't know."

"Never, are you sure? Not once?"

She is searching.

"When work around the house doesn't go right." A plaintive whine creeps into her voice. "Don't ask me any more questions."

"It's all over."

Again she grows calm, she is solemn, she is thinking, after a long moment of reflection this is the thought that she shouts out:

"Oh, how I'd like to show you my ingratitude, show you how ugly I am, how impossible it is to love me. I'd like to offer you that."

"You have offered it to me."

She lifts her head slightly, astonished at first, then suddenly grown old, deformed by some intense emotion which strips her of all her grace and delicacy and renders her coarse and sensual. I picture her nakedness next to mine, complete, for the first time oddly enough, in a rapid flash, just long enough to ascertain whether I would be able to bear it if that moment should ever come. Lol Stein's body, so distant, and yet so inextricably wedded to itself, solitary.

She goes on talking about her happiness.

"The sea was in the waiting-room mirror. At that time of day the beach was deserted. I had taken a very slow train. All the bathers had left the beach and gone home. The sea was the way it used to be when I was young. You were not in the town at all, even before. If I believed in you the way others believe in God I could ask myself: why you? Does it have any meaning? Yet the beach was empty, as empty as if God had not yet finished making it."

I in turn tell her about what happened two nights before in my room: I had studied my room closely, and I had moved various objects around, as though surreptitiously, according to the vision she would have had of them if she had come, and also according to her place among them, Lol moving among the unmoving objects. I pictured them being moved about into so many different positions that I became upset, it was as though some sort of unhappiness came and lodged in my hands because of my inability to decide what the exact position of these objects should be in relation to her life. I gave up the game, gave up trying to fit her, alive, into the death of things.

I continue to hold her as I tell her all this. I have to hold her forever, not let her go. She stays. She talks.

I understand what she wants to tell me: what I have been saying about the objects in my room has happened to her body, what I just said reminded her of it. She has taken it for walks through town. But that's no longer enough. She is still asking herself where this body ought to be, where exactly to put it, so that it will cease to be a burden to her.

"I'm at least a little closer to knowing than I was before. For a long time I used to put it somewhere else than where it ought to have been. Now I think I'm getting closer to the place where it will be happy."

By her face and by her face alone, as I touch it more and more urgently, roughly, with my open hand, she experiences the pleasure of love. I was not mistaken. I was looking at her from so close up. The full warmth of her breath burned my mouth. Her eyes are dead, and when they open again I see upon me for the first time the gaze of someone who has lost consciousness. She moans weakly. She says:

"Tatiana."

I reassure her.

"Tomorrow, I'll see her tomorrow."

I take her in my arms. We gaze out at the countryside. We come to a station. The train grinds to a halt. A small village nestles around a town hall, which has been recently repainted yellow. She begins to recall specific places.

"This is the next to last station before Town Beach," she says.

She is talking, talking to herself. I listen attentively to a slightly incoherent monologue, of no importance to me. I listen to her memory beginning to function, to take hold of the shapes which she juxtaposes one beside the other like some game, the rules of which have been lost.

"There used to be a wheat field there. Ripe wheat."
She adds: "Wha¹ extraordinary patience!"

It had been in this same train that she had departed from Town Beach forever, in a compartment like this one, with her family around her wiping the beads of perspiration from her forehead, offering her something to drink, making her stretch out on the compartment seat, her mother calling her my pet, my love, my beauty.

"The train used to pass this wood much farther away. There wasn't ever any shadow on the field, and yet there was bright sunlight. My eyes hurt."

"What about the day before yesterday? Was the sun shining?"

She didn't notice. What was it she saw the day before yesterday? I don't ask her. At present she is experiencing a mechanical series of successive recognitions of places, of things, these places and things, she can't be mistaken, we really are on the train to Town Beach. She is erecting a scaffolding which, it would appear, is temporarily necessary for her, a woods, a field of wheat, patience.

She is completely preoccupied by her effort to recognize things. This is the first time she has deserted me so completely. And yet, every once in a while, she turns her head and smiles at me like someone who has not forgotten, though I must not let myself believe it.

The distance is growing shorter and shorter, is forcing her to hurry, at the end she talks almost without interruption. I don't hear it all. I'm still holding her in my arms. When someone is vomiting, you hold him tenderly. I too begin to pay attention to these indestructible places, which at this moment in time are becoming the sites of my arrival on the scene. Now the hour of my entering Lol Stein's memory is at hand.

The ball will be at the end of the trip, it will fall like a house of cards, as this trip is presently falling. She is seeing her present memory for the last time in her life, she is burying it. In the future it will be today's vision she will recall, this companion beside her in the train. This trip, in the future, will be like the town of South Tahla is for her now, lying in ruins beneath her footsteps of the present. I say:

"I love you, so very much. What's to become of us?"

She says that she knows. She doesn't know.

The train is moving more slowly through a sunny countryside. The horizon is growing brighter and brighter. We are going to arrive at a region where the light will bathe everything, at an auspicious hour, the hour when the beaches empty, about noon.

"When you look at Tatiana the way you did the other evening, without seeing her, I have the feeling I'm remembering someone I'd forgotten. Tatiana at the ball. And then I'm a little bit afraid. Maybe I shouldn't see you together any more, except . . . "

Her words had come in a rush. Perhaps her sentence was left suspended because of the noise of the brakes beginning to be applied: we're in Town Beach. She gets up, goes to the window, I get up too, and together we see the seaside resort come into view.

It sparkles in the midday light.

There is the sea, calm, in different iridescent tints depending on the make-up of the bottom, a weary blue.

The train descends toward the sea. Suspended in the sky above is a layer of light purple haze, which the sun is in the process of burning away. We can see that there are very few people on the beach. The majestic curve of the gulf is colored by a broad circle of bath houses. The tall, white, regularly spaced street lights give the square the proud look of some broad boulevard, a strange height above sea level, urban looking, as though the sea had made inroads on the town since she was a child.

In the center of Town Beach, as white as milk, an enormous bird poised for flight, its two equal wings trimmed with balustrades, its overhanging terrace, its green cupolas, its green shutters lowered against the summer sun, its rodomontades, its flowers, its angels, its garlands, its gold, its milk-whiteness, as white as snow, as sugar: the municipal casino.

It moves slowly by to the high-pitched, drawn-out squeal of the brakes. It stops, completely visible now.

Lol laughs, jokes:

"The Town Beach casino, how well I know it!"

She leaves the compartment, pauses in the corridor, reflects.

"Promise me we're not going to stay in the station waiting room."

I laugh.

"I promise."

On the station platform, and in the street, she takes my arm, my wife. We are leaving our night of love, the compartment of the train. Because of what has happened between us, we can touch each other more easily, more intimately. I now know the full power, the sensitivity of this gentle face—which is also her body, her eyes, her seeing eyes are too—drowned in the sweetness of an endless childhood which floats just on the surface of the flesh. I say to her:

"I know you better since our train ride together."

She knows what I mean by that, she slows down, overcomes what seems to be a temptation to turn back.

"You are now part of this trip which people have kept me from taking for ten years. How stupid they were!"

As we leave the station she looks in both directions, hesitating which way to go. I start walking, taking her with me, in the direction of the casino, the better part of which is now concealed by the intervening buildings of the town.

Nothing is happening within her except a recognition of the sites, a formal, still very pure, unruffled recognition, a trifle amused perhaps. Her hand is in mine. The memory itself goes back beyond this memory, back beyond itself. She was perfectly normal once upon a time, before she went mad at Town Beach. What am I saying?

I say:

"This town is not going to serve any purpose for you."

"What would I remember?"

"Come here the way you came to South Tahla."

"Here is the way I came to South Tahla," Lol says again.

The street is wide and descends with us toward the sea. Some boys in bathing suits and brightly colored beach robes are walking up the street. Their complexions are all the same hue, their hair is slicked down by the salt water, they look as though they all belong to the same large family, to which they are going home. They bid each other good-bye, and each goes his separate way, after having agreed upon a time to meet later at the beach. Most of them disappear inside small, furnished one-story bungalows, leaving the street emptier and emptier, the farther we go up it. Women's voices shout first names. Children answer that they are coming. Lol stares with curiosity at her youth.

Without realizing it, we've arrived in front of the casino. It was there, off to our left a hundred yards away, set in the midst of a lawn which we had been unable to see from the station.

"What do you say we go to the casino?" Lol says.

A long corridor crosses it from side to side, one end of which opens onto the sea and the other onto the main square of Town Beach.

The municipal casino of Town Beach is deserted except for a woman in the cloakroom just at the entrance and a man dressed in black who is pacing the floor, his hands behind his back; he yawns.

Long dark curtains with a floral design on them cover all the exits, they stir constantly in the breeze that sweeps the corridor.

Whenever there is a gust of wind, one catches a glimpse of deserted rooms with closed windows, a gambling room, two gambling rooms, the tables covered with large sheets of metal painted green and padlocked shut.

Lol sticks her head into every opening and laughs, as

if she is enjoying this game of exploring the past. Her laugh is contagious and starts me to laughing too. She is laughing because she is looking for something she thought was here, something she therefore ought to find, but doesn't. She walks ahead, retraces her steps, lifts a curtain, pokes her head inside, says No, that's not it, no question about it, that's not it. She calls upon me to confirm her lack of success each time another curtain falls back into place, she looks at me and laughs. In the muted light of the corridor her eyes are shining, bright, clear.

She examines everything. Not only the posters announcing coming events, the gala evenings and the contests, but the display windows full of jewelry, dresses, and perfumes as well. Someone other than myself might have been taken in by her at this particular moment. I find myself the spectator of a display of gaiety both unexpected and irresistible.

The man pacing the floor comes over to us, bows to Lol, and asks her if he can be of any service, if she needs anything. Lol, taken aback, turns to me.

"We're looking for the ballroom."

The man is pleasant and helpful, he says that at this time of day the casino is, of course, closed. This evening at half past seven. I explain as best I can, say that all we want is a quick look, because we came here when we were young, just a peek in is all we'd like.

The man smiles sympathetically and asks us to follow him.

"Everything is closed. You'll have a hard time seeing."

He turns into a corridor perpendicular to the one

from which we have just come: that is what we should
have done. Lol has stopped laughing, she slows down
but continues to follow behind, dragging her heels.
And then we are there. The man lifts a curtain, we still
can't see, and he asks us whether we remember the
name of the ballroom, since there are, in fact, two in
the casino.

"La Potinière," Lol says.

"Then this is it."

We go in. The man lets go of the curtain. We find
ourselves in a fairly large room. Tables are set in a
circle around the dance floor. At one end there is a
stage with a red curtain, which is closed, and at the
other end a promenade with a border of green plants.
A table covered with a white tablecloth is there, long
and narrow.

Lol was looking. Behind her, I was trying to accord
my look so closely to hers that, with every passing
second, I began to remember her memories. I remembered events contiguous to those events she remembered having been present at, sharp profiles of similari-
ties that vanished the moment they were seen into the
dark night of the room. I heard the fox trots of an
uneventful youth. A blonde was roaring with laughter.
A couple—two lovers—came toward her, a slow-mov-
ing comet, the primary maw of love, she still didn't
realize what it meant. A sputtering of secondary inci-
dents, a mother's screams, occurs. The vast, dark field
of dawn arrives. A monumental calm reigns over
everything, engulfs everything. One trace remains,
one. A single, indelible trace, at first we know not

where. What? You don't know where? No trace, none, all has been buried, and Lol with it.

The man is pacing to and fro behind the curtain in the corridor, he coughs, he is waiting patiently. I move closer to Lol. She doesn't see me come. She cannot keep her eyes fixed for more than a moment on one thing, has trouble seeing, closes her eyes to see better, opens them again. Her expression is set, conscientious. She can spend the rest of her life here looking, stupidly seeing again what cannot be seen again.

We heard the faint click of a light switch, and the ballroom's ten chandeliers light up together. Lol gives a cry. I call out to the man:

"Thank you, but that won't be necessary."

The man turns out the lights. By contrast, the room is much darker than before. Lol leaves. The man is waiting behind the curtains, smiling.

"Has it been a long time?" he asks.

"Oh, ten years," Lol says.

"I was here."

His expression changes, he recognizes Miss Lol Stein, the indefatigable dancer—seventeen years old, eighteen—of the Potinière. He says:

"I'm sorry."

He must know the rest of the story too, I can see he obviously does. Lol hasn't the slightest inkling that he knows.

We have emerged through the main door out onto the beach.

We went to the beach without having made up our minds to. Once outside in the light, Lol stretched, yawned broadly. She smiled, she said:

"I got up so early this morning I'm sleepy."

The sun, the sea, the tide is going out, is out so far it has left behind a marshland of sky-blue puddles.

She lies down on the sand, gazes at the patches of blue water.

"Let's go and get something to eat, I'm hungry."

She falls asleep.

Her hand, lying on the sand, falls asleep with her. I toy with her wedding ring. Beneath it the skin is lighter, smoother, like a scar. She is completely oblivious. I remove the ring, smell it, is has no odor, I slip it back on. She is completely oblivious.

I make no effort to fight the deadly monotony of Lol's memory. I fall asleep.

She's still asleep, in the same position. She's been asleep for an hour. The light is more oblique now. Her eyelashes cast a shadow. A light breeze is blowing. Her hand is still in the same place as it was when she fell asleep, buried a trifle deeper in the sand, her fingernails are no longer visible.

She wakes up a moment after I do. There are very

few people on this part of the beach, here the beach is silty, people go swimming farther down, miles away, the tide is way out, ebb tide for the moment, beneath the screams and shrieks of the idiotic gulls. We study each other. We've known each other so briefly. At first we're astonished. Then we rediscover our current memory, our marvelous, recent memory of this morning, we move into each other's arms, let me hold her tight, we stay this way, not saying a word, there being nothing to say until, looking toward that section of the beach where the swimmers are and which Lol, because of the position of her head on my shoulder, cannot see, there is some commotion, a crowd gathering around something I cannot see, perhaps a dead dog.

She gets up, takes me to a little restaurant she knows. She is famished.

Here we are then at Town Beach, Lol Stein and I. We are eating. Another series of events might have taken place, other revolutions between people other than ourselves, with other names, other spans of inner time might have occurred, longer or shorter, other tales of oblivion, of a vertical descent into the oblivion of memory, of lightning-like access to other memories, of other long nights, of love without end, of God knows what? Lol is right. That does not interest me.

Lol is eating, gathering sustenance.

I refuse to admit the end which is probably going to come and separate us, how easy it will be, how distressingly simple, for the moment I refuse to accept it, to accept this end, I accept the other, the end which has still to be invented, the end I do not yet know, that no one has invented: the endless end, the endless beginning of Lol Stein.

Watching her eat, I forget.

There's no way we can avoid spending the night in Town Beach. We realize this while we are eating, and the realization affixes itself to us, clings to us, we forget there might have been any other possibility. It is Lol who says:

"If you like we can spend the night here."

She's right, we can't get back.

I say:

"Yes, we'll stay here. We have no choice."

"I'm going to telephone my husband. The mere fact that I'm in Town Beach can't really be sufficient reason for him to . . ."

She adds:

"Afterward I'll be so good and reasonable. Since I've already told him it was all over between us, I can change, can't I? I can, you see I can."

She clings to this conviction.

"Look at my face, you must be able to see it, tell me we can't go back."

"I can see it in your face, we can't go back."

In successive, steady waves, her eyes fill with tears, she laughs strangely, a laugh I have never heard.

"I want to be with you, you've no idea how I want to be with you."

She asks me to go and rent a room. She's going down to the beach to wait for me. I go to a hotel. I rent the room, I ask questions someone answers, I pay. I'm with her waiting for me: the tide is finally coming back in, it drowns the blue marshes one after the other until, progressively, slowly but surely, they lose their individuality and are made one with the sea, some are already gone, others still await their turn. The death of the marshes fills Lol with a frightful sadness, she waits, anticipates it, sees it happen. She recognizes it.

Lol dreams of another time when the same thing that is going to happen would happen differently. In another way. A thousand times. Everywhere. Elsewhere. Among others, thousands of others who, like ourselves, dream of this time, necessarily. This dream contaminates me.

I'm obliged to undress her. She won't do it herself.

Now she is naked. Who is there in the bed? Who does she think it is?

Stretched out on the bed, she does not move a muscle. She is worried. She is motionless, remains there where I have placed her. Her eyes follow me across the room as I undress, as though I were a stranger. Who is it? The crisis is here. An attack brought on by the way we are now, here in this room, she and I alone.

"The police are downstairs."

I don't dispute her words.

"People are being beaten on the stairway."

I don't dispute her words.

She doesn't recognize me, hasn't the faintest idea who I am any more.

"I don't know any more, who is it?"

Then she remembers me faintly.

"Come on, let's go."

I say that the police will catch us.

I lie down beside her, beside her closed body. I recognize the smell of her. I caress her without looking at her.

"You're hurting me."

I keep on. By the feel of my fingers I recognize the contours of a woman's body. I draw flowers upon it. Her whimpered resistance ceases. She is no longer moving, now doubtless remembers that she is here with Tatiana Karl's lover.

But now at last she begins to doubt that identity, the only identity familiar to her, the only one she has used at least as long as I have known her. She says:

"Who is it?"

She moans, asks me to tell her. I say:
"Tatiana Karl, for example."

Exhausted, at the end of my strength, I ask her to help me.

She helps me. She knew. Who was it before me? I shall never know. I don't care.

Later, shouting, she insulted me, she begged me, she implored me to take her again and in the same breath said to leave her alone, like a hunted animal trying to flee the room, the bed, coming back to let herself be captured, wily and knowing, and now there was no longer any difference between her and Tatiana Karl except in her eyes, free of remorse, and in the way she referred to herself—Tatiana does not state her own name—and in the two names she gave herself: Tatiana Karl and Lol Stein.

It was she who waked me.

"It's time to go home."

She was dressed, her coat on, standing there. She still looked like the person she had been throughout the night. Reasonable in her own way, since she would have liked to stay longer, she would have liked to begin all over again, and yet she decided she couldn't. Her eyes were lowered. She pronounced her words slowly, in a voice which was hardly more than a whisper.

While I am dressing she goes to the window, and I studiously avoid approaching her too. She reminds me that I am supposed to meet Tatiana at the Forest Hotel at six o'clock. She has forgotten a great many things, but not this rendezvous.

In the street, we exchanged looks. I called her by her name, Lol. She laughed.

We were not alone this time in the compartment, and had to talk in hushed tones.

At my request, she talks to me about Michael Richardson. She tells me how great a tennis buff he was, says that he used to write poetry that she found beautiful. I urge her to talk about it. Can she tell me anything more? She can. Each word is a shaft of pain wracking my whole body. She talks on. Again I urge her to continue. She lavishes pain with generosity. She tells me about nights on the beach. I want to know still more. She tells me still more. We are smiling. She's been talking the way she did that first night, at Tatiana Karl's.

The pain vanishes. I tell her so. She says no more.

It's over, truly over. She can tell me anything, whatever she wants to about Michael Richardson, about anything.

I ask her if she thinks Tatiana Karl is capable of informing John Bedford of our affair. She fails to understand the question. But she smiles when she hears Tatiana's name, at the memory of that small black head which is so far from realizing the fate that has been decided for her.

She does not talk of Tatiana Karl.

We waited until the last passengers had left the train before we left.

In spite of everything, I felt Lol's growing remoteness as something extremely difficult to bear. What? for no more than a split second. I asked her not to go home right away, told her it was still early, that Tatiana could wait. Did she even consider it? I doubt it. She said:

"Why tonight?"

Night was falling when I reached the Forest Hotel.

Lol had arrived there ahead of us. She was asleep in the field of rye, worn out, worn out by our trip.

PANTHEON MODERN WRITERS ORIGINALS

THE VICE-CONSUL

By Marguerite Duras, translated from the French by Eileen Ellenbogen

The first American edition ever of the novel Marguerite Duras considers her best—a tale of passion and desperation set in India and Southeast Asia.

"A masterful novel."—*The Chicago Tribune*

0-394-55898-7 cloth, $10.95   0-394-75026-8 paper, $6.95

MAPS

by Nuruddin Farah

The unforgettable story of one man's coming of age in the turmoil of modern Africa.

"A true and rich work of art...[by] one of the finest contemporary African writers."
—Salman Rushdie

0-394-56325-5 cloth, $11.95   0-394-75548-0 paper, $7.95

DREAMING JUNGLES

by Michel Rio, translated from the French by William Carlson

A hypnotic novel about an elegant French scientist and his shattering confrontation in turn-of-the-century Africa with the jungle, passion, and at last, himself.

"A subtle philosophical excursion embodied in a story of travel and adventure...It succeeds extremely well."   —*The New York Times Book Review*

0-394-55661-5 cloth, $10.95   0-394-75035-7 paper, $6.95

BURNING PATIENCE

by Antonio Skármeta, translated from the Spanish by Katherine Silver

A charming story about the friendship that develops between Pablo Neruda, Latin America's greatest poet, and the postman who stops to receive his advice about love.

"The mix of the fictional and the real is masterful, and...gives the book its special appeal and brilliance."   —*The Christian Science Monitor*

0-394-55576-7 cloth, $10.95   0-394-75033-0 paper, $6.95

YOU CAN'T GET LOST IN CAPE TOWN

by Zoë Wicomb

Nine stories powerfully evoke a young black woman's upbringing in South Africa.

"A superb first collection."—*The New York Times Book Review*

0-394-56030-2 cloth, $10.95   0-394-75309-7 paper, $6.95

THE SHOOTING GALLERY

by Yūro Tsushima, compiled and translated from the Japanese by Geraldine Harcourt

Eight stories about modern Japanese women by one of Japan's finest contemporary writers.

"Tsushima is a subtle, surprising, elegant writer who courageously tells unexpected truths."   —Margaret Drabble

0-394-75743-2 paper, $7.95